TROUBLE JOINS THE PHOENIX TEAM

Scott Gideon had assembled his Phoenix underground team to get maximum strike force. There was Brusilov, a huge Russian bear of a man . . . Wladyslaw, a handsome, daring Polish pilot . . . In'Hout, a Dutch Jew burning for vengeance . . . Kinelly, an irreverent Irish adventurer . . . Charvey, the embodiment of the shining idealism and brutal realism of France.

But now someone new had linked up with this select company. Her name was Eliska Dobrensky, as expert with a gun as she was exciting with her body. Gideon couldn't trust her, but he also couldn't turn her down. For only she could guide him and his men to the castle of Count Laszlo, the mysterious nobleman who was her lover and her master—and who held the lives of the Phoenix team in his elegant and ruthless hands. . . .

MAGYAR MASSACRE
RESISTANCE #2

More SIGNET Action-Adventure Series

RESISTANCE
THE MAGYAR MASSACRE
2

GREGORY ST. GERMAIN

A SIGNET BOOK
NEW AMERICAN LIBRARY
TIMES MIRROR

PUBLISHER'S NOTE

This novel is a work of fiction. Names, characters, places, and incidents are either the product of the author's imagination or, if real, are used fictitiously.

The first chapter of this book appeared in *Night and Fog*, the first volume of this series.

SIGNET TRADEMARK REG. U.S. PAT. OFF. AND FOREIGN COUNTRIES REGISTERED TRADEMARK—MARCA REGISTRADA
HECHO EN CHICAGO, U.S.A.

SIGNET, SIGNET CLASSICS, MENTOR, PLUME, MERIDIAN AND NAL BOOKS are published by The New American Library, Inc., 1633 Broadway, New York, New York 10019

First Printing, October, 1982

1 2 3 4 5 6 7 8 9

PRINTED IN THE UNITED STATES OF AMERICA

1

HE WAS SHIVERING violently; his head throbbed with pain and a steady roar was pulsing in his ears.

He groaned and shifted his legs. Then, after what seemed like a long time, he identified the noise. The roaring was outside his head. It was the sound of fast-running water.

Returning to consciousness opened the gates to his memory. He was Scott Gideon, an American, the leader of Phoenix. The next image was the mountains, the foothills of the Ukrainskaja Karpaty where they had delivered the general to the Polish resistance forces gathered there. And finally, he remembered the new mission assigned to Phoenix that had brought them to this godforsaken patch of rugged Ruthenian terrain.

In March of 1939, Hitler had wiped Czechoslovakia off the map. The Hungarian government had jumped into bed with the Nazis in order to grab Ruthenia, the mountainous territory lost by Hungary following the Great War. Then the Fascist-leaning government of Hungary had confiscated a fortune in artwork, gold, and silver from Slovak aristocrats who opposed the annexation of their homeland. The treasure was to be shipped to Germany as part of the tribute exacted by Hitler for allowing Hungary to seize the territory. And Phoenix, in cooperation with a group of those aristocrats whose goods had been seized, was to recapture the treasure and transport it to Western Europe. The aristocrats' spokesman, the influential Count László, had agreed with Monsieur Philaix that the treasure would then be sold, with half the proceeds going to purchase arms and supplies for a fledgling Hungarian resistance movement.

Over the crackling radio that was the prize of the nascent Polish forces, Gideon had briefly detailed the success of the first Phoenix mission to Philaix. The wealthy Belgian industrialist who had founded and bankrolled the commando team listened without comment to Gideon's explanation of the rescue of the prominent Polish general and resistance leader from a heavily fortified Nazi prison in Kraków, and his safe delivery into the hands of the Polish nationalists gathered in the mountains south of Kraków. As memory returned, Gideon wondered for a moment how he and his men would have been expected to complete the mission—and contact Philaix—had not the first men to come upon the forced-landing site of their leaky Russian IL-2 plane been well-armed resistance fighters. When Gideon finished, Philaix had simply said, "Good work," and launched into the explanation of the next Phoenix exploit.

But the Phoenix team from its conception had been a wild, almost foolhardy gamble, based on the same weapons—treachery and sabotage—that Hitler had employed so effectively. Henri Auguste Philaix was a true aristocrat, stern, haughty, powerful, with superb connections throughout the Continent. The shrewd judgment that had made him rich convinced Philaix of the monstrous folly of Britain and France in trying to appease Hitler. Philaix believed the Nazi leader wouldn't stop until all of Europe had been ground under the jackboots of German troops.

Committing his own personal wealth, Philaix had organized the Phoenix team of highly trained commandos who would penetrate into occupied countries, to link up with the patriots who refused to collaborate with the Nazis and their puppet governments. Their goal: a ground swell of armed resistance that would repeatedly strike at the ravenous Fascist beast from within. The team had started with eight men from every walk of life, handpicked and trained by Philaix in France; the number had dwindled to the present six, with the American Gideon as leader.

Gideon opened his eyes. Above him was the lean face of Joel In'Hout.

The Dutchman smiled. "For a while we didn't think you were going to make it."

"I didn't either," Gideon said. He started to rise, but In'Hout pushed him gently back down.

"You stay quiet for a while," In'Hout said. "That was quite a blow you took on your head."

Gideon's awareness of the throbbing at his temples was renewed. "Where are we? What time is it?" he asked, rubbing his head, the pain intensified by the sound of the rushing water; he now saw he was lying on the bank of the swollen stream.

"It's about midnight," In'Hout said. "We're downstream from where we tried to cross—on the other side this time. But we're not out of the woods yet; Brusilov lost the raft when he dove for you. We need dry clothes, food, weapons. We saved only four pistols; yours was lost and Brusilov's was soaked."

Gideon had hoped that this trek through the remote, wild country between the Polish resistance camp and their destination in Hungary—the castle of Count László in Petrescaba—would provide the team with a much-needed respite. But first had come three days of torrential downpours that had chilled and exhausted them. In attempting to ford a swollen stream, Gideon had been swept downstream when a log racing on the icy water had struck him with enough force to detach him from the human bridge formed by his men. The handmade raft on which their packs, recently replenished by the band of Poles, had been stashed had apparently been swept away too. The last thing Gideon remembered before losing consciousness was his swift progress toward a black outcropping of rock.

"Brusilov got me out?" he asked. In'Hout nodded. Gideon didn't need further explanations; the massive Russian bear of a man had already proved his strength repeatedly since they set off for Poland in late January of

3

1940, a few short months ago but months packed with a lifetime of fighting and death.

A gust of wind came up, sweeping across Gideon's soaked clothing. He shivered violently in the freezing air. "What about a fire?"

"We didn't want to risk it. Brusilov and Kinelly are out scouting now. I gave Brusilov my pistol."

Since the Magyar takeover, guerrilla bands of Slovaks had taken to the hills, vowing to resist the seizure of Ruthenia. Gideon believed the Hungarian army was now sweeping the hills to flush out partisans. If the Phoenix team were discovered, they would be killed with no questions asked. Yet they desperately needed supplies in order to continue the mission . . .

"Ian and Charvey?" Gideon asked, straining his eyes to search the dark, hilly woods surrounding them.

"They went further downstream to see if they could salvage anything of our packs. They'll be back soon; it's too dark to see worth a damn."

Gideon grunted and lay back on the ground, resigned to waiting; for what, he wasn't sure.

The twisting, roundabout route squirreled up the side of a steep knoll and disappeared down into a grove of trees. The two men had reached the top and started to descend when Brusilov, in front, suddenly halted.

"Look," he said to Kinelly, pointing up to the crown of the trees.

Against the panorama of bright stars they could see a wispy thread of smoke rising from somewhere in the grove.

"Let's check it out," Oscar Kinelly said, his voice with its marked Irish accent dropping to a whisper.

The two men began easing from the rocks toward the grove. They slowly circled around through the scrub and tall grass to enter the grove on the side away from the road. Then, keeping in the deeper darkness of the trees, they wormed their way along a culvert and up a shale bank.

It was a hard climb. Their muscles, already exhausted by the arduous stream crossing, strained to keep hold in

4

the gravelly, crumbling shale. They were forced to move inches at a time, in order to keep as quiet as possible. When they finally crested the bank, they lay on their bellies on the ridge, breathing shallowly through their mouths.

As their breathing normalized, they stared down into a little clearing that jutted off the side of the road. Twenty-five or thirty men were grouped around a campfire, eating dinner. They all wore the khaki uniform of the Royal Hungarian Army, with its pointed-crown side cap and single-breasted tunic. They also wore the breeches and boots and blue insignia patches of a cavalry brigade, a fact confirmed by the whinnying of horses from an area beyond two supply wagons parked at the far edge of the clearing.

"Giddiyup troops," Kinelly murmured contemptuously.

"Not so fast should you dismiss them," Brusilov cautioned. "In wild hill country such as this, a mounted squad is far more effective than motorized troops."

"You think they're looking for us?" Kinelly asked.

Brusilov shrugged. "Gideon thinks the army was hunting down the Slovaks. Whether or not they are on our trail doesn't make much difference. They will still kill us."

Kinelly started to raise himself to get a better look.

"Down!" Brusilov hissed, thrusting a hand against Kinelly. "Keep flat. The moon is bright enough to see our silhouettes against this ridge. And they must be crack shots with those Mannlicher rifles of theirs."

"To hell with their rifles," Kinelly growled. "What I want is that food. I can smell meat cooking and . . ."

Kinelly paused in midsentence as he heard a horse approaching along the road. They watched as the cavalry mount galloped into the light of the campfire. The rider reined in sharply and dismounted in a jump. One of the men rose from around the fire and accepted the rider's hasty salute; the man must have been the squad leader, maybe a sergeant. He stood with his hands clasped behind his back, nodding as the rider spoke and gestured up the road.

"Damn!" Kinelly spat. "They must have tracked us."

Brusilov shook his massive bald head. "If they had

found the others, we would have heard shooting. But I wish I knew what that rider was saying."

The rider stopped talking. Then the squad leader turned to bark orders at the rest of the men. The squad hastened to obey, swiftly packing kits and weapons. They moved off into the shadows toward the horses, and within moments a fast-trotting double line was heading north up the road. Left behind was a detail of six to guard the supply wagons.

"Just our luck," Kinelly whispered. "They didn't all go."

"If they had, they would have taken the wagons with them," Brusilov pointed out. "As it is, maybe we can get the drop on them without having to get into a fire fight. With only pistols, we can't afford a shoot-out."

"Let's go," Kinelly said. "I'm ready to eat one of those horses, I'm so starved." The quick temper and impatience that had bounced the Irishman out of the British navy was barely in check.

"We've got to wait for the squad to ride out of hearing range. And just in case that messenger is leading the squad to In'Hout and the others, we've got to be able to get back there fast."

The minutes crept by, seemingly endless. No noise, no sudden flurry of gunfire, erupted behind them.

"All right," Brusilov said at last.

The two men slithered down over the rise toward the clearing. At a hand signal, Kinelly angled off toward the right. Brusilov, amazingly stealthy for one his size, elbowed and kneed through the scrub and tall grass. Soon the two commandos reached the edge of the clearing, about ten yards from each other. They lay on their stomachs, surveying the scene.

The Hungarian soldiers had their rifles leaning upright against the wagons, obviously unaware of approaching trouble. Three of them were sitting around the fire, and the other three were lazily reloading cooking equipment into the supply wagon on the far right.

Brusilov started to raise his hand to signal Kinelly to attack. Before he could motion, one of the soldiers stood up and began to saunter directly toward them. Both men

6

flattened and kept perfectly still, listening to the footsteps. The soldier started to angle toward Kinelly. Brusilov held his breath, hoping that in the darkness the Irishman wouldn't be seen.

The Hungarian stopped within a pace of Kinelly and began unbuttoning his fly. Brusilov watched helplessly as the soldier loosed a thick stream of urine into the thicket.

With an infuriated snarl, Kinelly reared up, a dripping specter. There was a startled intake of breath from the soldier. Then Kinelly punched him square in the face, knocking him flat.

Instantly, Brusilov was up and running. Kinelly leaped over the comatose soldier and joined the rush. The five remaining Hungarians swiveled, then for a moment froze, gaping.

"*Álljon meg!*" Brusilov shouted, "stop" being about all the Hungarian he knew. "*Álljon meg!*"

Two Hungarians by the campfire desperately fumbled for their pistols in their waist-high flap holsters. One squeezed off a round from his Roth-Steyr. The shell whizzed by Brusilov's ear. The Russian triggered his Walther P38, and the soldier's body jerked and writhed, pistol dropping from nerveless fingers.

The other soldier had started to raise his weapon when Brusilov crashed into him with lowered shoulder. The impact sent the soldier flying. He slammed into the side of the supply wagon, then slumped to the ground. Brusilov shot him once through the temple.

Kinelly had drilled one of the three men who had been loading the other supply wagon on the right side of the clearing. But the other two had reached their weapons and were pouring out a hail of rifle fire. The ground around Kinelly's feet churned as he dashed past the still-blazing campfire and dove behind the wagon where Brusilov crouched.

The impact of his dive temporarily knocked the wind out of him. Brusilov knelt by him with concern. Kinelly signaled with a nod that he was unhurt.

For a moment the firing stopped. Brusilov moved to the corner of the wagon, then stuck his head out cautiously. A shell whacked into the wooden side of the wagon an inch above his head. He ducked back.

"*Bozhye moy!*" Brusilov hissed. "In the light of that campfire, they can see everything."

"The fire will die," Kinelly said.

"We cannot afford the time. God knows if that mounted patrol heard the firing."

Brusilov looked around for a moment. Then he spotted a water barrel next to the wagon. He creeped alongside and found it was three-quarters full.

He motioned to Kinelly and hurriedly explained his plan.

"You'll never lift that," Kinelly said.

Brusilov glowered at him. "You be ready."

Brusilov put down his pistol, then crouched by the barrel. His long arms barely reached around its thick waist. He breathed deeply, clenched his teeth, then began to lift.

For a long moment he strained in vain. His cheeks bulged, his arms ached, his immense thigh muscles started to knot. He relaxed for an instant, then pulled again.

In one incredibly swift motion he stood. He staggered for an instant, getting his balance. Then he started out from behind the wagon toward the campfire ten feet away.

When he came into the open, the two remaining Hungarian soldiers opened fire. A bullet tore through his trouser leg, and three more slammed into the barrel, which started to slip. Brusilov managed one more step, then deliberately fell, bringing the barrel down with him.

The thirty gallons of water gushed out, quickly dousing the flames. The soldiers stopped firing for the briefest of moments. It was enough. They were still gaping when Kinelly opened fire from behind.

One soldier fell instantly. The second managed to turn and fire a shot. Then the rifle barrel started to drop and a second bullet hit the ground at his feet. Kinelly stepped up close and shot him again, between the eyes.

Brusilov was at his side a moment later. "Quick," he said. "Go back and get the others while I harness horses to one of the wagons."

"Why not ride horseback?" Kinelly asked.

8

"We can't stay here long enough to eat and select and pack supplies. Besides, Gideon may not be able to ride. Hurry."

Without another word, Kinelly moved off to climb back up the bank toward the ridge. Brusilov led two of the four draft animals back and hitched them to the tree of the nearest wagon.

Once the wagon was ready to go, he made a cursory study of the supplies, making sure foodstuffs and canisters of ammunition were in the bed. He then scoured the campsite, gathering the weapons of the slain camp guards and tossing them into the wagons with their backpacks and bedrolls.

He was saddling a couple of cavalry mounts when Kinelly returned with the rest of the team. Brusilov broke into a broad smile when he saw that Gideon was with them and walking unassisted.

Gideon came up and shook his hand. "Good work," he said.

Brusilov nodded, "We are not free yet. We seem to have declared war on Hungary, all by ourselves."

2

THEY HEADED SOUTH, keeping the pace at a steady trot in order to save the horses. The Frenchman Charvey and Ian Wladislaw, the quick-witted young Pole who at nineteen was the youngest member of the team, rode the saddle mounts. Gideon knew enough rudiments of horsemanship to ride bareback on one of the spare draft horses, as did Kinelly, who had grown up on a farm. Brusilov alone had been trained in handling a brace and wagon, so he drove, with In'Hout sitting next to him.

They ate as they rode. The foodstuffs were regulation army fare, edible only to those on the verge of starvation. To the ravenous Phoenix team, they tasted delicious. They forced themselves to save enough of the tinned meat, beans, and crackers for another meal. What they did eat restored some of their energy and made the cold mountain wind easier to bear.

Capturing the wagon and horses so quickly had been a fortunate break. But they were still in great danger. The Hungarians could easily pick up the trail and pursue them with everything they had. Their only chance was to build distance before daylight, when they could be spotted from the air.

After they'd eaten, Gideon rode up to the wagon to talk to Brusilov. "We can't risk the road for very long," he said. "As soon as we get a little lower, out of the worst of these hills, we'll cut southeast cross-country. We may just have to ride to the border and slip into Rumania to get away."

"That's more than a day's ride," Brusilov said.

"What other choice do we have? We're way outnumbered and outgunned."

Brusilov picked up one of the Mannlicher M95 rifles they had captured. "At least we have these," he said. "There are far worse things than to stand and fight." A white Russian, Brusilov had been with the White Army at its last stand against the Bolsheviks.

"Then drive well," Gideon said with a smile. He nudged his mount and rode up ahead.

The road sloped downward for miles. When it started to level off, dawn was approaching, and the sky was slowly turning from black to smoky-blue. In this faint light, Gideon saw that they had arrived at a long rolling expanse of meadowland. The dark shapes of forested slopes seemed to ring it on three sides, but toward the south the flatter land spilled out as far as the light allowed them to see. The road meandered in an increasingly western direction, away from where they wanted to go.

Gideon's decision wasn't difficult; this was a good place to try cutting cross-country. He signaled to Brusilov, then led the way off the road. They dipped through a series of fields, skirting thickets and groves, then angled along a gentle slope to the floor of a bowl-shaped valley.

From the valley, they entered a stretch of rougher country, hills and canyons and intersticed ravines which forced them to slow to a walk. Ahead, silhouetted in the first rays of the rising sun, were the spires of a mountain range too far away to be visible when they first left the road.

Gideon wasn't pleased when the flatter land dropped abruptly into a shallow canyon that ran southeast to the nearest foothills of the range. They followed the canyon, which grew increasingly narrow, until the sides pressed together and formed a bottleneck hardly wide enough for the wagon to pass.

"We have to turn back," Brusilov called out.

Gideon pondered, then replied, "I hate the idea of do-

11

ing that. We've got to get cover soon, before full light. At least we're going in the right direction. Let's stick it out."

With the help of Gideon and Kinelly, Brusilov managed to squeeze the wagon through the bottleneck. The canyon beyond widened again. They came to an S-curve, and rounding the double bend, they saw that the canyon continued for another couple hundred yards, then ended. Dead end.

"*Merde*," muttered Charvey in disgust.

Gideon cursed himself for not scouting ahead and saving precious time. Then he dismounted and called to the other men to help turn the horses and wagon around in the narrow space.

A single shot sounded from the cliff above the bend. Charvey, Ian, and Kinelly heeled their mounts into a gallop. Brusilov lashed the reins and yelled at his horse, and the wagon rocked high and lurched from side to side as it rattled ahead with Gideon, remounted, at its side. They cleared the last yardage of loose rock, dismounted at the rear of the canyon, and scrambled on foot into a small pocket formed by boulders, carting as many weapons and ammunition canisters as they could.

After a moment's rest, Gideon moved the team to a position higher up the canyon wall, where they had clear firing lines down the canyon toward the bend. In'Hout and Kinelly moved out to the left, stacking small rocks to improve their defense. Charvey and Ian climbed up to the right, to a point beyond a flat slab of rock. Charvey hummed to himself as he worked the bolt of his Mannlicher and sighted it.

Gideon and Brusilov checked their own rifles, then distributed the spare cartridge clips to facilitate reloading. They crouched behind two small boulders to wait.

Brusilov muttered under his breath as the time passed, and Gideon rubbed his inner thighs, chafed raw by his long bareback ride.

Finally, Kinelly called up to Charvey, "See anything?"

Charvey shook his head.

Gideon turned to Brusilov. "I'm beginning to think that shot wasn't aimed at us."

Brusilov nodded. "I was thinking that, too. Above the

12

bend may have been a lone advance scout, one of many sent out to search. We worked it like that when I was fighting the Bolsheviks."

"I did the same thing in Spain. If one of our scouts came across an enemy force we could hit, he'd dog it until they camped. Then he'd summon the brigade."

Despite a Quaker upbringing, Gideon had enough of the rebel in him to have fought in the Spanish Civil War until a stray bullet had ended his service. An expert in explosives, he'd been listlessly pursuing chemistry studies in Brussels when he spotted Philaix's call to arms—a cryptic ad in the international *Herald Tribune*. Philaix had made Gideon the leader of Phoenix, as his American nationality gave him judgment unclouded by sentiment on European soil; Gideon's calm under fire had been well tested in Spain.

Stretching out, propping his rifle against his knees, Gideon said, "The only problem is, this guy was able to signal with a shot. That means the main body of troops must be damn close. And we're trapped."

"He's only one."

"One's enough," Gideon replied. "If we tried to run it, he'd pick us off like so many clay pigeons before we could clear that double curve, much less the bottleneck."

"If this had only happened an hour earlier, when it was still dark," Brusilov said.

"That would have given us a chance to slip away," Gideon agreed. "Now all we can hope is that for some reason—"

He stopped as Brusilov nudged him.

Softly at first, then louder, they heard the echoing ring of iron on stone. Horses were approaching. Soon, rounding the bend, rode shadows black against the snow-silted rock. An exact count was impossible, but Gideon guessed there were twenty men fanning out between the boulders. And he was willing to bet there was another group circling through the hills to the rim of the canyon behind them to cut off their escape upward.

"Get ready," Gideon called out hoarsely to his men. He stretched flat and pressed his cheek against the rifle stock. Looking down the rear sight and through the clamp-on

13

front sight protector, he gauged the attackers as they slowed their pace and began easing cautiously through the rocks toward the team's line of fire. He began squeezing the trigger.

Kinelly's shot beat him by a split second. The bullet struck inches from the nearest rider, then richocheted, whining through the canyon. The man dove from his saddle as Gideon and the rest of the team opened up with a fusillade of bullets, emptying their five-cartridge clips in a single savage burst. The result was confusion below, as men leaped to their feet and scrambled for cover, their mounts milling wildly and galloping back toward the bend with empty saddle skirts bouncing.

The attackers began returning fire. Then, one by one, they advanced from boulder to boulder in an attempt to flank and close in. Gideon rammed in a magazine and picked off a man breaking into the open on his left. Another followed, too quickly to shoot, and vanished behind new cover.

Gideon caught peripheral movement off to his right. He hastily nudged Brusilov. "There."

In one lightning-swift motion Brusilov sighted and fired. He winged the soldier in one leg, but the man managed to crawl into a depression out of sight before Brusilov could fire again.

Gideon looked to his left. In'Hout was sniping at a pair of men angling toward his fortified position, keeping their advance to a snail's pace. Above, Charvey and Ian were laying down a steady stream of fire to pin four or five attackers in a large clump of boulders.

In return, the team was taking heavy fire from the canyon floor. The bullets bounced off rocks and slugged into the canyon walls, their reports resounding upward.

Soon, however, the level of fire declined as the assault was stymied. The attackers contented themselves with a stalemate for the time being, with occasional forays to deplete the besieged defenders' dwindling supply of ammunition.

As Gideon inserted a fresh clip in his weapon, he turned to look upward to the rim of the canyon. This was

14

dead country, bare, cold, pitiless. He calculated they had another half hour before troops worked their way . . .

His heart skipped a beat as he saw three black silhouettes appear against the brightening sky.

Brusilov saw the expression on his face. "What is it?"

"They got here faster than I thought," Gideon said grimly.

Brusilov looked skyward to see the movement along the rim. He looked back at Gideon. "At least they're not behind us yet. Another fifteen minutes, maybe."

"That means we have a chance," Gideon said.

"To see if we can take them first."

"Right," Gideon said. Quickly, he issued orders.

Gingerly, the team began edging up the rear slope of the canyon, using every rock and boulder, every slight depression. Then, from the right side of the canyon rim, came a wink of flame and the slap of a bullet close by Gideon. He rolled and fired, then wormed upward to a jumble of rocks. Brusilov crawled beside him. They waited for another flash of gunfire to sight in on, but could only catch fleeting glimpses of more figures moving into firing position.

"There must be as many men up there as there are down in the canyon," Brusilov said.

"Yeah," Gideon said, rubbing his forehead. The pain from the fierce rap he'd taken when swept against the rocks crossing the stream had subsided to a dull ache during the long ride. Now it was again like a dagger twisted in his skull.

He closed his eyes, breathing deeply, forcing, by will, the pain from his mind. Then he opened his eyes and said, "If the odds are even up and down, I guess we ought to choose down."

There was a look of determination on Brusilov's face. "Bad odds either way," he said grimly. "Do me a favor, Scott." The huge Russian looked straight into Gideon's eyes.

"Sure."

"Save a round for me. If I go down first. I will not be a prisoner."

Gideon nodded, then turned and crawled over to tell each of the men of his decision.

They listened with the cool detachment of professionals. Gideon had just moved away from Ian when he heard Charvey call out, "I cannot believe it!"

Gideon whirled. Below, walking slowly out from under cover, were two men dressed in nondescript clothing. One man had his hands raised to show they were empty; the other carried a tall stick with a white shirt as a flag.

"They can't be surrendering," Ian said.

"Maybe they want to talk," Gideon said.

"It's a trick," In'Hout commented.

Gideon shrugged. "What do we have to lose? Cover me."

After the intense skirmishing, the absence of gunfire was eerie. Gideon stood, slowly handed his rifle to Charvey, then descended toward the canyon floor.

As the two men approached, Gideon saw that the one holding the flag was a large, ruddy-faced brute wearing dirty butternut trousers, a fleece-lined coat, and steel-capped boots. The man with his hands raised was shorter and more wiry, and wore an ill-fitting brown woolen suit. He was also older, with bushy white eyebrows and wisps of hair peeking from beneath a stained snap-brim hat. And, most amazingly, he was smiling, as if he were greeting a long-lost comrade instead of an enemy.

"*Dobrý večer*," he said. "Good morning. Can you understand me?"

Gideon recognized the language as Slavic, but he couldn't get the meaning. The man repeated his greeting, but Gideon indicated by gestures the language difficulty.

Then Ian appeared by Gideon's side. He said to Gideon, "If the man is speaking Czech or Slovak, I should be able to understand. They're both very close to Polish."

"Go ahead," Gideon said.

Ian introduced himself in Polish.

The man beamed. "I am Xaver Neruda, and these are my men. Do you understand me?"

"Yes," Ian said. "If you go slowly."

"I will," Neruda said. He fished a metal flask from his

16

inside jacket pocket. Unscrewing its cap, he extended it to Gideon. "Maybe a sip of *slivovice* would warm you, my friend?"

Ian translated. Gideon shook his head no, and asked, "What do you want?"

"To end this misunderstanding." Neruda took a hefty swig of plum brandy, wiped his mouth on his sleeve, and continued, "We believed you were Hungarians, despite assurances from the man who traced you here that you weren't in uniform. It was the horses and wagon that misled us."

Ian, searching for the right words, took a moment to translate. Gideon said nothing, not understanding the drift of the man's conversation.

Neruda chuckled. "Ah, but five minutes ago, I received word of the ambush of the Magyar motor patrol and the massacre of cavalry troops. Immediately I realized that you must be, as the news broadcasts have been saying, foreign agitators and enemies of the state. Naturally that means that whoever you are and whatever you're doing here, we are brothers after the same cause."

Ian translated, and the import dawned on Gideon. He told Ian, "Ask him if he's telling us that they are Slovak partisans. Resistance fighters."

"*Ano, ano,*" Neruda replied, nodding his head, his smile broadening. "Patriots, my friend, fighting against the aliens who have usurped our land." He jiggled the flask invitingly. "*Promiňte*? Please, now we toast to friendship?"

After hearing Ian's rendering of the speech, Gideon debated, then took the flask and raised it. "*Na vaše zdraví*! To your health!" The fiery brandy scalded his throat and exploded in comforting warmth in his stomach. Teary-eyed, he returned the flask.

"Let me talk to my men," he said through Ian.

Neruda nodded.

Gideon and Ian climbed back up the slope and gathered the team around him. Gideon quickly related the conversation.

"Do you believe him?" Charvey asked. A trade unionist before joining Phoenix to fight the Nazis on his own terms, the Frenchman could be depended upon to proceed with care in negotiating.

"I believe he's Slovak," Gideon said. "And if we could mistake them for Hungarians, I suppose they could do the same for us."

"What's the bloke after?" Kinelly asked. "What does he want from us?"

"All he's offered so far is a drink."

Kinelly snorted. "That's a good start."

"I hope he'll help us get the hell out of here," Gideon continued. "But we're going to be totally helpless if—"

"Excuse me," Neruda called. "As one warrior to others, I do not want to hurry you. But with the report of your heroic deeds came the report that the Hungarian Ninth Army is not far behind. I and my men, we can swiftly fade into the hills. We can hide you."

After Ian translated, Gideon turned back to his men. "You heard him. I think this calls for a vote. Brusilov?"

The Russian nodded yes.

"Kinelly?"

"I could use a drink."

"In'Hout?"

The Dutch Jew's thin face was grim. "I don't like his looks."

"You're not going to marry him," Charvey said, "I vote yes. And the kid does, too."

Gideon looked over to Ian, who didn't protest.

"All right," Gideon said. He rose and with Ian at his side, walked back to Neruda. He reached out and took the flask from the Slovak and took another swig of the scalding liquid. "We accept your offer."

"You will not regret it," Neruda said. He looked upward. "Come," he called.

The team eased down the slope, rifles held in the crooks of their arms, wariness still in their eyes. Neruda's men rose from their positions on the canyon floor and began circling in, grinning, laughing, shaking hands and thumping backs. It didn't take long for the team to lower their rifles and reach out for the numerous proffered flasks. With the warm feeling in the gut provided by the brandy came an equally warm sense of relief.

18

After a few more minutes of camaraderie, Neruda offered his flask to Gideon again, saying, "A final swallow before we go?"

"No thanks. I've had enough."

Neruda tilted the flask, drained it, then smacked his lips. "In that case, I must now ask you and your men to raise your hands." He was beaming as he spoke. "You are all under arrest."

3

WAKING IN THE gray of a dreary dawn, lying on a cold stone floor, Gideon thought that once the stale, fetid air of a jail stings a man's nostrils, the remembrance never fades.

The stench grew as the light strengthened and the foul air began to warm. Cautiously, to avoid stepping on his friends, Gideon eased across the tiny cell to the small iron-barred window set into the massive old walls. He stood there staring out, gratefully inhaling the fresher air.

Before him stretched the motley collection of houses, barnyards, and inevitable manure piles of a little farming village. It was empty at this early hour except for a stray mongrel sniffing around.

Yesterday morning, when Gideon and the rest of the Phoenix team had been marched into town, every man, woman, and child had been lined up to catch a glimpse of the "foreign agitators." The indignity of their capture by the peasants of this tiny, remote village galled Gideon. He seethed with bitterness and self-recrimination that as leader of Phoenix, he had led his men into this.

His men, however, didn't blame Gideon in the least. Even Brusilov said he preferred this dank, cold cell to the even colder mountain ground in which their bodies would almost certainly have been buried had they chosen to try to fight their way out of that canyon. The Russian pointed out that the police building was far from a fortress and that their cell hadn't had to accommodate more than an occasional petty thief or drunk in centuries. He thought their chances of escape were excellent.

So far, however, no chance whatsoever had presented itself. When they had first reached the police building, Neruda had tried to interrogate them. But he soon grew impatient with Ian's limited ability to act as interpreter. Neruda gave up in disgust, slamming the thick wooden door that led from the narrow corridor running along the barred cell to his office.

Since yesterday morning, that door had opened only once. The sullen, hostile brute who had carried the phony truce flag at the canyon had brought them coarse black bread and wedges of pale goat cheese. For drinking water, the Slovak had left a pail with a ladle just outside the bars. He hadn't opened the cell door at all, not even so that the slop bucket could be passed out for emptying. That bucket, now nearly full, was a major contributor to the foul air that had made it so difficult for Gideon to sleep.

It was now fully light outside, and the rest of the team began to stir. Joel In'Hout joined Gideon at the window.

"A long night," In'Hout commented. He inhaled deeply, exhaled, then turned to Gideon. "All night I had one ear listening for the sound of the Hungarian army trucks coming to take us away. But dawn finds us here."

"I don't understand that," Gideon said. "I can't see why else they would have locked us up."

"I know," Charvey called out. "Their woman have finally demanded real men instead of goat herders. As we were marched in, I saw some well-constructed young wenches eyeing me."

"Marcel, the way you smell now, you wouldn't attract a goat," Kinelly scoffed. "As for me, I would shake hands with an Englishman to get a quart of that fiery brandy. At least that would take off the chill."

"I could use that brandy, too," Brusilov said. He stretched his arms, yawning. Then he added, "We will talk to the maître d' when he serves our breakfast. I am sure . . ."

Brusilov paused as he heard a key in the lock of the wooden door. "Speaking of the devil," he said.

But the hands of the Slovak brute were empty. And following him into the narrow corridor were Neruda and a man dressed in a black suit with a clerical collar.

"Mon dieu!" Charvey exclaimed. "A priest. He has come to give us the last rites, before we are shot."

"Mais non," the priest said in lightly accented French. "Your lives are not in danger at the present."

"You speak French," Gideon said in amazement.

The priest smiled wryly. He was a thin, almost gaunt man with unruly sandy hair and pale skin. His age could have been anything from thirty to forty-five.

"Yes, I speak French," the priest said. "I am Father Présoc. I was in Mukačevo yesterday visiting a patient at the hospital when you were brought in. Today, I am here to interpret for your interrogation."

"Your job is over," Gideon said. "I have nothing to say."

"On the contrary," Father Présoc said. "I believe you have a lot to say. Sheriff Neruda certainly has a lot to say to you. He will alternately threaten and cajole, while you will fence and parry and bargain. Don't worry, I will handle that end for you."

"I don't understand," Gideon said.

The priest smiled again. "I am sorry. What I mean is that Neruda will think I'm faithfully translating. While he's thinking that, we can talk."

"About what?"

"About what you're doing here. And . . ." The priest's voice trailed off as Neruda tapped him on the shoulder. He patiently listened to a long speech in the Slovak dialect, then turned back to Gideon.

"As I was saying," the priest said. "I can tell you much. For example, many of the men in this village are true patriots who hate the Hungarians and were shamed to participate in your capture. But in this part of the world no man dares to question his village leader."

"What's the story with Neruda?" Gideon asked. "Why is he keeping us locked up?"

The priest turned to talk to the sheriff, listened, then said to Gideon, "Neruda is a vain, stupid man who recognizes that things have changed. The Hungarians have come through even this remote village to conscript young men and to take livestock and food. In you and your men, Neruda believes he has found a great prize with which he can barter with the Hungarians, just as he barters for horses with other villages. Like any horsetrader, he wants to question you first to find out your true worth. What he doesn't realize, of course, is that once you are handed over, the Hungarians will forget all promises and punish him and the village for audacity."

"Why don't you tell him that?" Gideon said. "Convince him to let us go."

The priest pursed his lips. "I am afraid I have limited influence. We have quarreled constantly. Neruda is not a spiritual man."

Gideon waited for the priest to conclude another exchange with the sheriff. Then he asked, "What is a man who speaks French as well as you doing in a place like this?"

Amusement flickered in the priest's eyes. "You think I am a spy? I wish it were so. I was a scholar, a teacher in a seminary, and I studied in Paris. However, I am also a man, and not a very lucky one. Considering in whose bed I was discovered, I was fortunate that my punishment was only banishment to this village."

Gideon pondered for a moment. Then he asked, "Why are you telling me this? What can you do for us?"

"I would like to help free you. If you could tell me who you are, what you are doing, if you have any friends on the outside, I can be of help. I am anxious to be of help."

Gideon studied the priest.

"I know you have doubts after what you have been through," Father Présoc added. "Discuss it with your men. Neruda will expect you to talk over his drivel."

Gideon turned around. "You heard him," he said. "What do you think?"

The men stood in silence for a moment. Then Ian, whose French was very poor, said, "I did not follow the conversation well. But you're the leader. We'll leave it up to you."

"I didn't do so well the last time," Gideon said.

"You did the only thing you could do," Brusilov said. "And this time you will do the only thing you can, also."

Gideon looked at Brusilov for a moment, then nodded. He turned back to the priest and asked, "Does the name László mean anything to you?"

Shock registered on the priest's face. At the same time, Neruda's smile vanished. He grabbed Father Présoc's shoulder and barked at him.

Their exchange lasted a long time before the priest said to Gideon, "Do not utter that name again. I finally convinced him that what he heard was *l'oiseaux*, the French word for 'birds.' "

"I don't understand."

"The person you mentioned is the head of the oldest and most powerful noble family in Ruthenia. He is the most outspoken of patriots, and tying him to you and your men would give Neruda some real bargaining power."

Gideon leaned forward. "We are on our way to perform a vital service for . . . for the man we are discussing. You must send a messenger to him at once."

"I can do better than that," the priest said. "I have a shortwave radio, with which I can reach all points in Europe. Without that radio, without communication to the world I left, my life would be nothing. I will get a message out immediately."

"That's wonderful," Gideon said. "But—"

"I am afraid we must conclude this," the priest said. "Neruda must not get suspicious. I've bought you some time. You can expect another interrogation this afternoon."

The hours of their second day in the tiny jail cell crept by at a snail's pace. Gideon was sitting on the hard floor, his back against the wall, dozing, when Ian called him to the window.

Gideon reached his side in time to see a stately gold-and-black dinosaur of a car make its way into the cobbled square in front of the police building. The car was an early-30's German Maybach V-12, with an elongated hood, an open-air seat for the chauffeur, an enclosed pas-

24

senger compartment the size of a living room, and two spare tires overhanging the square trunk like a stubby tail section.

The car passed out of view of the small cell window.

"László?" Ian asked.

"I hope so," Gideon said. "Let's be ready."

The limousine pulled to a halt in the middle of the square, beside a crude statue of the village's founder. A group of curious children flocked around the car, while the faces of women appeared in windows and doorways, hoping to get a glimpse at whatever lofty personage must be riding in so grand a vehicle.

Neruda and his huge bodyguard appeared on the steps of the police building just as the immaculately uniformed chauffeur, a well-built young man, opened the door to the passenger compartment. To their amazement, the person who emerged was a tall, strikingly beautiful woman in her late twenties. The woman had auburn hair clipped short in the current fashion, large brown eyes, full lips and flawless, unrouged skin. A full-length gray wool coat masked her figure, but as she walked toward the police building she gave the impression of being slim-hipped and lithe.

As she approached, Neruda took off his snap-brim hat and bowed, his usual broad smile on his face.

"Good day, madame," he said.

"Good day," she replied. Her voice was cool and aristocratic.

"May I be of assistance?" Neruda asked. "Perhaps madame is lost?"

"I would like to go inside," she said in a tone that was more of a command than a request.

"I am afraid this building is to be used for official business only," Neruda started. "And at the—"

"I am here on business," the woman said. "And I am not accustomed to discussing my business in public."

"I see," Neruda said, nonplussed. He pondered for a moment, then smiled again. "Of course, madame," he said. "But my humble office is small, and perhaps your—"

She turned to her chauffeur. "Anton, you may wait with the car."

25

As the chauffeur bowed and retreated, she turned back to Neruda. "Now, if you please . . ."

The sheriff stepped back to let her pass.

His office was no more than a cluttered cubbyhole, with a beat-up wooden desk buried in paper and two ancient wooden chairs. Neruda pointed to a chair. The woman sat.

"Now, if I may help you?" Neruda asked.

"Two nights ago a band of armed foreigners attacked my estate, taking with them a quantity of gold coins and jewelry. I understand you have captured a group of foreigners."

Neruda swallowed, then smiled more broadly to mask his surprise. "Foreigners?" he said. "We have no foreigners, do we, Kalmath?"

The big brute standing in the doorway said, "No."

The woman didn't acknowledge his answer. "I am here to identify them. The jewelry included invaluable family heirlooms."

"I said, madame, that we have no foreigners here," Neruda insisted, an edge to his voice. "And I would appreciate knowing your name and where you are from."

"I am here to question you," the woman snapped. "Not to be questioned."

Neruda was taken back. He hesitated, then started, "But madame, I . . ."

The woman got to her feet. "If you did capture foreigners, your responsibility would be to turn them over to the Hungarians. I will send my chauffeur to verify the transfer with the local army commander."

Neruda blanched at the mention of the Hungarians, and got to his feet. "Wait, madame."

"Yes?"

Neruda's mind was racing fast, trying first to figure out how the news of the capture had traveled. That concern began to fade before the subject of the stolen gold coins and jewels. He'd been searching for a way to profit from the situation, and he might have found it.

His manner suddenly became more courtly. "Madame, I have in custody men who may in fact be foreigners. I am in the process of conducting a thorough interrogation.

26

When that is completed, I will be delighted to let you know what I have found."

Her expression grew more stern. "I want to see them now."

"But—"

"Perhaps the Hungarians should handle this after all."

Neruda sighed. "All right, madame. I warn you, as a lady, that the smell—"

"Show me to them."

Neruda gestured to Kalmath, who unlocked the wooden door.

The woman walked past him into the narrow corridor.

Charvey's mouth dropped in amazement. *"C'est une femme!"*

The woman looked them over.

"Well," Neruda said, "are these the men?"

The woman stepped closer to the bars and said in English, "Which one of you is Gideon?"

For a moment Gideon was stunned by her perfect South Kensington accent. Then he replied, "I am. Who are you?"

"We have been waiting so anxiously. The time is so short."

The conversation taking place in the unrecognizable language troubled Neruda greatly. "No interrogation," he said forcefully.

The woman turned to face him. "You will set these men free now," she commanded.

Neruda's face darkened with anger. "I think possibly you should join them," he said.

He motioned to Kalmath, standing next to him. The brute took a menacing step forward.

Calmly, the woman took her hand out of the large pocket of her coat. In the hand was a Luger. She aimed and pulled the trigger.

The bullet entered the huge Slovak's mouth, blowing out the back of his skull. He crashed to the floor.

Neruda was frozen in shock for an instant. Then he took a step backward, saying, "No, please, no . . ."

The woman shot him twice in the chest, the impact slamming him against the wall of the corridor.

"Incroyable!" Charvey exclaimed.

The woman quickly took the cell key from the belt of the dead jailer. She unlocked the cell door and stepped back. "This way," she said. "Hurry."

The men followed her. When they got to the sheriff's office, Gideon said, "Wait. We need weapons."

The Mannlichers and Roth-Steyr pistols taken from them were stacked in a corner, along with their ammunition. Brusilov bashed open a locked wooden cabinet and his face lit up.

"An MP40 machine pistol!" he fairly shouted. "Our luck is changing."

"Come," the woman said. "We must hurry. They will be after us."

4

ALL BUT A handful of the men of the village were in the mountains with their flocks when the team emerged from the police building. The chauffeur was standing outside the car, Luger in hand, motioning them onward. They raced across the square, sensing eyes watching them from the windows, and dove into the Maybach's huge passenger compartment. The chauffeur rammed the gearshift into the first of the car's eight gears and tromped on the gas. The Maybach lurched ahead, back tires squealing. As they accelerated down the road and around a curve, shots whined over their heads.

"Boy," In'Hout exulted, "how nice it is to be out of that cell."

Gideon turned to the young woman. "First of all, we'd like to thank you. And we'd also like to know to whom we owe the favor."

"I am Eliska Dobrensky, secretary to Zsigmond László."

"Obviously a man of good taste," Charvey remarked, his eyes focused on the delicate line of Eliska's graceful neck.

The beautiful woman's expression remained serious. "These are terrible times. Our Ruthenia has been occupied and looted by the bandit Hungarians, who are in turn lackeys of the Nazis. Quick death is too kind for traitors like those two animals back in that village."

"It is rare, such passionate hatred in a woman," Charvey remarked.

She turned to him, her eyes flashing. "Women can hate and fight as well as men. My brother was killed by the Fascists, my parents imprisoned, our family's property and estate confiscated. My only hope is the hope of all Ruthenian patriots, Count László."

"We're looking forward to meeting him," Gideon said.

"We were concerned about your delay," Eliska said. "Through informers we heard of the attack on the cavalry squad and the massive search being conducted by the Hungarians. You were fortunate to end up in the hands of the villagers instead."

"How far do we have to travel?" Gideon asked Eliska.

"Nearly fifty kilometers," she replied. "But on these muddy, winding roads, it is like a trip twice that far. Fortunately, we are traveling down out of the mountains, which will—"

At that moment, two Hungarian open military cars chugged around the bend and headed toward them.

The chauffeur slammed on the brakes and twisted the steering wheel to the left. The limousine skidded to a stop on the muddy shoulder.

The Hungarian vehicles slowed momentarily, then accelerated. The soldiers in the rear seats sprayed rounds of carbine fire at the Maybach V-12. A slug caught the chauffeur under the right arm as he stepped out of the car. He staggered, then fell.

In'Hout, Charvey, Ian, Kinelly, and Eliska tumbled out the left-hand door and scrambled toward the trees. Brusilov hurriedly checked his weapon. As the first military car came level with the limousine, he stepped out the door and raked it with a long burst from his German machine pistol. The windshield exploded. The driver and front-seat passenger arched backward in their seats. The car careened to the right, hit a rock, and plowed into a ditch.

Two men were still alive in the car. "Cover me," Gideon yelled to Brusilov as he sprinted across the road. He waited until he was ten feet away, then fired from the hip at full run. The closest Hungarian's head was blown off his shoulders in a cloud of disintegrating skull. The second man was trying to scramble out the side of the vehicle. When he saw Gideon, he started to raise his weapon. Gideon fired, and the man's stomach opened up before he hit the ground.

The second Hungarian car had pulled up next to the limousine. The soldiers were using it as cover to pin the other members of the Phoenix team. They were unaware of Gideon and Brusilov at their backs until the Russian sprayed one with his MP40. The other three ducked for cover between the military car and the limousine.

"Dammit!" Gideon spat. "I'd give anything for a grenade."

Brusilov grinned. "I do not think we will need it. Watch."

He jammed another clip into the machine pistol, then stood. Impervious to the bullets whizzing by him, he fired off a long burst that stitched the side of the Maybach.

"What in the hell are you doing?" Gideon shouted.

An instant later, the gas tank of the limousine exploded. Brusilov dropped, slamming Gideon into the mud. Jagged sections of metal from the vehicle few over them, and they felt a wave of intense heat. A moment later the military car also exploded.

They held their hands over their heads as mud, gore, and metal rained down on them. Then, abruptly, all sound and movement ceased. Gideon got to his knees and used his hand to wipe the thick coating of muck from his face. Then he stood and called out, "Charvey?"

"I am all right," came the answer.

"Kinelly?"

"We're all fine, for chrissakes," the Irishman growled as he climbed up to the road and inspected the burning ruins of the Maybach. "But I wish I could say the same for our fancy car."

Eliska came up to Gideon. "It is fortunate the Hungarians were surprised to encounter us."

"On equal terms, no soldiers are a match for Phoenix," Gideon said. After the embarrassing capture by Neruda, he couldn't resist lavishing praise on his men.

"I hope you are right," Eliska replied. "Your test will soon come."

Gideon turned away, thinking, What a cold one. He'd never met a woman so controlled.

A shot rang out.

Gideon dropped to his knee, bringing his rifle automatically into firing position. Then he saw Brusilov standing over a body with a pistol in one hand. Gideon exhaled, lowered his weapon, and walked over to him.

"What happened?" he asked.

Brusilov pointed with the pistol. "This one was still alive. One of the first things I learned as a boy fighting with General Denikin against the Bolsheviks—always search with a pistol loaded and ready."

Gideon nodded his approval, paused to look around for a moment, then called out, "Let's get the hell out of here before they come looking for these guys."

"They already are," Ian commented.

"What do you mean?"

Ian pointed upward. It took Gideon a moment to spot the twin-engined airplane flying low over the canyon toward them.

"Hungarian," Ian said. "A WM-21 reconnaissance craft, probably."

"Cover!" Gideon shouted.

They scrambled for the rocks. The whine of the plane grew louder as it passed overhead. The noise started to fade, then picked up again as the pilot made a second pass.

The men waited until the sky was silent before they emerged.

"Shit," Gideon muttered. "They'll be up our ass before we know it." He asked Eliska, "Which way should we go?"

"On foot, we have only one choice. Up there."

The team was at the edge of a natural bowl of steeply terraced rock. Above, a rocky escarpment rose toward a cliff.

"The queen's ass, I'm climbing that," Kinelly spat.

"It's your ass if the Hungarians get here," Gideon said He glanced at Eliska, pointing at her elegant garments and high-heeled shoes. "How are you going to climb in those?"

"I'm not," she said. "If a couple of you can help. I'll get the pants and boots off one of these soldiers."

Once again Gideon was impressed by her calmness and level head. "Charvey, Ian," he ordered.

Charvey smiled broadly. "I am always at the service of a mademoiselle who needs help dressing."

The rest of the men gathered spare ammunition clips while Eliska quickly changed. Then they moved out, Brusilov leading the way.

The sharpness of the shale that formed the terraces tore their hands. But that turned out to be the easy part. The soil of the boulder-strewn slope above had been turned to muck by the recent rains. They half walked, half crawled upward, slipping a step back for every two or three they took.

After a half hour, Gideon's legs felt as if somebody were stabbing him in the thighs with an icepick. The knees of his rugged pants were torn completely through, and sweat poured down his forehead in such volumes that his eyes stung from the salt. He was struggling more than Eliska, who kept pace with the team with quiet determination.

Finally, he signaled for a rest. The team members collapsed. It was a few minutes before Gideon summoned the strength to pull out his canteen and take a long drink of water.

Somewhat refreshed, he turned to look downward. He was still staring when he heard Brusilov's heavily accented voice. "Gideon."

"What is it?"

"The cliff, up there." Brusilov pointed. They were two-thirds of the way up the escarpment, a couple hundred yards below a sheer wall of granite that rose abruptly toward the sky. "Where do we go?"

"I don't know," Gideon said. "But we can't turn back. Look."

He gestured toward the road. Two trucks had reached the wreckage from the fire fight, and soldiers swarmed over the nearby rocks like ants.

Brusilov grunted. Without a word, he picked up his

pack and his weapon and started out. The rest of the team followed.

The adrenaline from seeing how close the pursuit was drove them at a faster pace. In half an hour, they reached the cliff, then made their way along it as they tried to circle the mountain. They slowed as the slope on which they walked became steeper. Ahead, it seemed to disappear completely, melting into the mountain to become one huge straight granite wall.

Gideon called a second halt. He went on to reconnoiter, putting off for a moment the seemingly inescapable decision to turn around and fight it out with the numerically superior soldiers.

Then he found it. A rock chimney, cut into the cliff over the ages by a trickle of water that even with the heavy rains of the last days wasn't large enough to call a stream. It was a wide vertical crack in the granite face, four feet wide at the bottom, then narrowing near the top, fifty or sixty feet above. Gideon couldn't tell whether it was wide enough for a man to slip through. But they had to find out.

Gideon hurried back to the team and led them to the crack. The only man whose face didn't reflect doubt was In'Hout, a former champion gymnast.

The Dutchman turned to Gideon and smiled. "This is more my cup of tea," he said. "I'll go first. I'll take a rope up with me."

"You read my mind," Gideon said.

In'Hout braced his shoulders and back against one wall of the chimney, then bent his knees, placing the soles of his boots against the opposite wall. He then literally walked up the cleft, depending upon the strength of his buttocks, thighs, and calves to maintain pressure to keep from falling. He took small steps, not relaxing one foot to scrape it upward until the other was firmly planted. At the same time, he walked his shoulders alternately, right, left, right, left.

As the chimney narrowed toward the top, In'Hout's legs became increasingly bent until he had to apply pressure with his knees instead of his feet. He reached up over the lip with both hands, feeling around to get the best possible grip. Then he dropped his legs. For one anxious second he hung, feet dangling, before he pulled himself slowly up and over the cliff's lip.

A minute later, he had untied the rope from his waist and fastened it securely around a large boulder. He hauled up the equipment and weapons of the men below.

Eliska climbed next, followed by the men. The only problem was Brusilov, whose massive shoulders became wedged in the narrow opening at the top. He clung to the rope for nearly ten tense minutes while the others pulled and shifted him. Finally, he popped through, the skin on the outside of both of his upper arms torn, and his shirt wet with blood.

The high winds of three hours earlier had signified a weather front moving through. Clouds now blown away, the sky above was blue as a robin's egg. The members of the team sprawled on the rock ledge, basking in the first warmth they'd felt for days.

Gideon wanted them to move on before the adrenaline stopped pumping and fatigue set in again. By moving now, they'd conserve more daylight for overcoming any further obstacles to getting off this mountain and away from the pursuing Hungarian troops.

He was about to give the order when Ian cried, "My God!"

Gideon's eyes shot skyward. A Hungarian fighter was spearing in toward them like a gleaming knife from the blue blanket of sky.

The team broke into a desperate run, aiming for a pile of boulders a hundred yards away. The fighter dove at them with a roar of horsepower and a whining staccato of spitting bullets. Charvey, who had almost reached the rocks, suddenly spun and toppled awkwardly to the ground.

Ignoring his own safety, Kinelly pivoted and dove after him. A bandage covering a week-old head wound started to unwind. As Kinelly ran, its unraveling tail floated behind him like a bloodstained gauze streamer. Barely slowing, Kinelly stopped and grabbed Charvey's arms, dragging him the last few yards to the boulders.

Ian was almost the second casualty. Lead plucked at

35

his left pantleg, and another round burned a gouge along the side of his leather belt. Heedless, he kept moving in a straight line.

The team crouched behind the boulders. Gideon looked out to see the fighter, high above the slope, circle in preparation for another strafing run.

"Like ducks in a shooting gallery," In'Hout said.

Gideon spotted Ian frantically waving from behind a small shale fall on the other side of the clump of boulders.

"I've found cover," Ian yelled. "Come."

"Let's go," Gideon said.

The roar of the diving fighter was deafening. Gideon sprinted hard, his head pounding, the team running behind him. He saw Ian pointing to a narrow, dark wound in the granite cliff.

"In here," Ian shouted.

The fighter opened fire just as Gideon threw himself on the ground, tearing up the palms of both hands. Hurriedly, he scooted like a lizard into the blackness.

A few feet beyond, the tunnel opened into a cave. Gideon turned and helped pull the men in behind him. The deadly rattle of machine-gun fire on the ledge outside echoed frighteningly.

Gideon waited a moment, then called out, "Is everyone all right?"

"All inside," Ian said, "barely."

"Is anyone hit?"

"Only Charvey," In'Hout said.

"How is he?" Gideon asked.

"I am all right," Charvey spoke up. "A flesh wound, that is all."

"Good," Gideon said.

"Good?" scoffed Kinelly in his thick Irish brogue. "We've crawled into our own damn tomb. All they have to do is seal us up."

"He is right," Brusilov said. "We cannot even fight our way out of that entrance."

"We may not have to," Ian said.

"What do you mean?" barked Kinelly.

"I've done caving, with my brother Stash. I believe this is a big system. And I hear water."

"So?"

"It is water, over the many centuries, that created this cave. That water must also have an outflow."

"You mean—" Gideon started to ask.

"If we follow the water, we may find our way out."

"I don't like this," Kinelly groused. "The Lord only knows how long we'll be wandering around in this infernal mountain."

Eliska spoke. "We know what we will find outside that entrance—the Hungarian army and air force. Even if they do not find this cave, they will search for days. We must reach the castle of Count László by morning. The train for Yugoslavia will depart in less than forty-eight hours. The treasure must be seized by that time and loaded on that train."

Gideon sighed, then said, "I guess we don't have any other choice." He turned to Ian. "You lead the way."

"I need light. We have to make torches."

"No, you do not," Brusilov said. "Learn this from an old soldier. I took an electric torch from those soldiers."

He removed the flashlight from his pack and handed it to Ian. Ian flicked it on, then started down the narrow, seven-foot-high rock corridor. After a hundred yards, the cave widened dramatically. When Ian flashed the light upward, they saw they had entered a natural gallery as large as an opera house. From the vast space, myriad arms and branches seemed to go off in all directions.

"*Mon Dieu!*" Charvey exclaimed in awe. "It is incredible."

"Incredible, my ass," muttered Kinelly. "It's a fucking maze, and we're the rats."

Ian listened, then said, "The water seems to be flowing to our left. We'll go that way."

In silence, the team crossed the gallery, then moved in single file down a slanting cut. The floors and walls of the cut had been scrubbed clean by the action of the underground stream, revealing the structure of the cave system. Above, the rock was limestone. Slowly, the slightly acid water had penetrated the porous material and eaten it away, making a path for itself. Finally, the water had gotten down to the level of the hard igneous rock on which they walked.

For more than an hour, Ian led the way along a corridor that narrowed steadily as they descended. Soon they were easing along a shallow ledge twenty feet above a rushing current of water. The roof continued to close in on them, until they were bent over double, their packs scraping the rock above.

The more the walls closed in on them, the more the unspoken thought formed in their heads: We've made a dreadful mistake; we're heading for some chasm or dead end. Yet no one spoke, even to grumble, as if unwilling to disturb the eerie darkness through which they bore.

The tunnel began to curve slowly to the right. Then suddenly the rock ledge was blocked by a spear of rock protruding out over the stream.

Gideon peered over Ian's shoulder as he flashed the torch. They couldn't see around the rock.

"Can we let ourselves down into the water and swim around?" Gideon asked.

Ian shook his head. "Too dangerous. Caves are full of vertical swallows. In the dark, we could be sucked down two or three hundred yards and smashed to death."

"So we have to go back?"

Ian was silent for a moment. Then he said, "Our only chance is to take it as we did the rock chimney. Help me get my pack off."

The tunnel had narrowed to four feet, the width of a small closet. After Ian's pack was off, he took out the rope and tied an end around his waist. He faced the stream and let himself fall forward to the other side. He caught himself with his hands, then turned so his back was against the wall. Then he walked his feet up the opposite wall, until he was braced between the two walls in a sitting poisition, about three feet above the ledge, as In'Hout had been braced when he climbed the rock chimney.

Only Ian was moving sideways instead of up. He wriggled to his right, sliding his shoulders and feet inch by inch under the projecting spear of rock, the stream roaring beneath him. His progress was achingly slow.

Gideon stood holding the torch, watching. What if the cut widened on the other side? Ian would be gone in an instant, and their very slim chances of getting out obliterated.

When Ian returned, he reported, "There's a fresh rock ledge, Gideon let out a sigh of relief. Ian called out, "We'll get the packs across first."

Soon the packs had been transferred, and they made their way around the spear one by one, using the rope as a railing.

In'Hout was the last. He untied the rope, then traversed the distance without assistance, just as Ian had.

When In'Hout reached the other side of the spear, Ian had already gone ahead to scout.

When Ian returned, he reported, "There's a fresh rock fall ahead. The slope is wide, but we have to be careful. The rock is rotten and loose, and a slip could mean a very long fall."

"We'll follow," Gideon said. "You've been terrific so far."

They moved out. For the next half hour, they picked through the rubble, making their way around often precariously balanced slabs of rock. The stream had disappeared, the water filtering its way below them.

Then, once again, they began to hear the sound of rushing water, at first low, then rapidly building in volume.

"The stream must re-form down there," Ian said. "Then we can follow it to—"

He gave a sudden, startled yell as the rock gave way under his feet. He flapped his arms, trying futilely to regain his balance. Then he fell, and started to tumble.

Gideon dove. He grabbed Ian's ankle, holding on tight as they slid slowly downward.

Then powerful hands grabbed and held Gideon from behind.

"Careful," Ian called out. "There's a dropoff."

Slowly, Brusilov pulled Gideon back. Moments later. Ian was on his feet.

"That was close," Ian said. "I would have been a

39

goner. And the torch would have been lost, so you would have been trapped in the dark."

"Nice thought," Gideon said. "What are we facing?"

"If you can find a secure spot to anchor, you can belay me. There's a ledge about twenty feet below."

"We'll find the spot."

Twenty minutes later, they were all standing on a broad, smooth, easy-to-follow rock ledge next to the stream.

"You think this leads out of here?" Gideon asked.

Ian smiled. "I'm almost sure of it. We must be down near the base of the mountain by now. It's just a matter of following the stream to the opening."

"Let's do it," Gideon said.

They followed the stream for a few hundred yards. For the first time since they'd entered the cave system, they talked among themselves as they made their way down the smooth but occasionally slippery-wet shelf. The prospect of breathing fresh air again and seeing the stars of what must now be the nighttime sky above was exhilarating.

Then Ian called a halt. Gideon moved up next to him.

The ledge ended in a small chamber, the size of the dining room at Philaix's Belgian chateau. The rock on which they'd been walking extended to the far wall of the chamber, making up half of its surface. The other half was a glimmering pool of water.

A jolt of alarm rocked Gideon. "Is this the end?"

Ian knelt by the pool, the surface of which was strangely still. He squatted, then put his hand to the water. When he stood, he turned to Gideon and said. "Do what I just did."

Gideon stared at him for a moment, puzzled, then knelt and put his hand into the cold water.

It was amazing. There was a strong pull on his fingers. Up close he could see that the water wasn't flat, but slightly bowed by the powerful suction. The water was so clear he could see, even in the inadequate light, a square opening six or eight feet below the surface, through which the water must be drawn.

Gideon stood and faced Ian. "Could we have made a wrong turn somewhere?"

Ian's face was solemn. "This is it. Down through that water is the channel that leads outside."

"What about going back? Can we—"

"We'll never make it," Ian said. "For one thing, we've nearly exhausted the battery on the torch. We'd be trapped somewhere up past that dropoff, on that fresh rock slope, in the pitch blackness. It wouldn't be a pleasant death."

"Then what do we do?" Gideon asked.

"The outlet from the mountain could be as little as forty or fifty feet down that channel," Ian said.

"Or?"

"Or it could be a lot longer. A man can hold his breath for two or three minutes. That current is so powerful it could carry a man a long way in that time."

"If he's not smashed to death," Gideon said. "And what if the outlet is four or five or six minutes away?"

Ian just grimaced.

Gideon called the now silent team together to explain the situation. At the end he said. "I think it's fair that we draw lots to see who goes first."

"Like hell we will," Kinelly growled.

"What do you mean?" Gideon asked sharply.

"Before the bloody Limeys kicked me out of their blasted navy, I was in submarine training. We practiced escaping from a drowned sub, and if I can't hold my breath longer than any man here, I'll kiss King George's balls."

"Are you sure? You don't—"

"Besides, if I have to spend one more minute in this fucking cave, I'll drown myself anyway."

Gideon took a minute to make up his mind. Then he said, "You're the man, Oscar."

They tied the rope around Kinelly's waist, after he'd removed his gear. He stood at the edge of the pool.

"Feet first," Ian instructed. "And hold on. That's all I can tell you."

Oscar turned to Gideon. "Three pulls on the rope— that means I've made it."

Gideon held out his hand. "Good luck."

Kinelly looked at it for a moment, as if deciding, then reached out and grasped his hand. Then he took three deep breaths, held the last one, and jumped.

He disappeared like a rock. Gideon continued to stare at the pool, unconsciously holding his breath at the same time.

It seemed like an eternity. Gideon's stomach was knotted, and his chest began to ache. All the time, the rope played out quickly, until the coil almost disappeared.

Then the rope stopped. The men pressed forward, watching. A minute passed, then another.

Gideon glanced at Ian, afraid to voice the thoughts racing through his head.

There was a tug on the rope. A second followed, and a third. Spontaneously, the men cheered, the roar echoing in the chamber.

The sense of relief was as overwhelming as each man's desire to get out of the oppressive cave.

Gideon issued orders. "Brusilov, you're next. Then Charvey, Eliska, In'Hout, and Ian. I hate to do it, but we're going to have to leave our packs and rifles behind."

"What about the pistols?" Charvey asked.

Gideon looked to Ian.

"You can tuck them in your belts," Ian said, "If you get stuck, well . . ."

The men knew what he meant.

The huge Brusilov swallowed gallons of air, circled his arms around the rope that would serve as a guide, then jumped.

In what seemed like a far shorter length of time than the wait for Kinelly, the "all's well" signal came.

Fifteen minutes later, Gideon was alone.

That he was the leader wasn't the only reason he wanted to go last. He didn't want the men to see his terror.

From the time he was a boy, he had hated the water. As a child, even swimming lessons occasioned in him a totally irrational but equally overwhelming panic. Later, with an incredible effort, he had taught himself to swim.

42

But he'd never been able to get used to going under the water, even for a moment.

As he stood in the pitch-black chamber, alone, he could feel himself trembling. He fought against the fear, knowing it would sap precious strength he would need later. For an instant, a vivid image of his own death flashed through his mind.

He took a deep breath and jumped.

The sensation was like jumping out of an airplane. In an instant he was sucked through the opening and whipped along a rock channel.

He reached a wider point, and the suction seemed to lessen. That settled his nerves as he seemed to float along. This isn't bad, he thought.

That was his last clear image. The current grabbed him again as it plummeted into a narrow channel. His foot hit something, his leg crumpled, his knee striking his chest. Then he spun and wedged sideways in the opening.

The water was roaring past him, and the need for air seared his lungs. He tried desperately to push himself free, but even moving an arm was an incredible effort.

The awful moment was an eternity. The pressure built in his chest and his throat convulsed. It was all he could do to fight the urge to open his mouth.

Then his shoulder loosened. The only way to get free was head first. He dove in the direction of the current, once more rocketing along.

The pain in his lungs was overwhelming. If he didn't reach the air in seconds, he knew he was a dead man.

He shot around a bend. He caught a flash of light and white foam ahead. Just before he was about to black out, his head broke through the surface, and he drank in the fresh night air.

5

THE CASTLE LÁSZLÓ, an immense medieval structure complete with turrets, battlements, and drawbridge, was cut into a rocky cliff overlooking a broad valley.

Huddled in the back of a horse-drawn cart, Gideon stared up through the gray, frigid, early-morning air at the forbidding structure. He said to Eliska, "I've seen friendlier-looking prisons than that."

"It was meant to look hostile and impregnable," she replied. "For centuries this region was torn by war, and no man could rely on his ruler's armies for his own defense." She sighed, then added, "Unfortunately, even in our modern age, that is still true."

Next to her, Kinelly shifted uncomfortably. "I don't give a damn how the building looks," he said. "I just hope to hell it's got hot water. I don't think I'll ever get warm again."

"I know what you mean," Gideon said. He was shivering, hungry, and exhausted. After the Phoenix team had emerged from the cave, they had traveled on foot nearly thirty kilometers through the rough, wind-swept terrain, still dressed in their soaking wet clothing. They had barely been able to put one foot in front of the other when they had reached László's estates. Eliska had awakened a farmer, who was bringing them the rest of the way in his horse-drawn farm cart.

Exhausted as they were, the severe bouncing of the cart and their bone-deep chill prevented them from sleeping.

44

So they sat, huddled under coarse horse-hair blankets, watching the castle grow closer and closer.

Finally, the cart halted between two fierce-looking eagles carved in stone that flanked the front end of the lowered drawbridge. The men jumped out, stretching their stiff muscles. Then they followed Eliska across the drawbridge to the huge metal-covered door.

The door opened as they approached. They walked through a small reception hall to a larger entrance hall, where they were met by a man wearing a smocklike white coat.

"Is the count awake, Vilém?" Eliska asked in Slovak.

"He has been up all night," the man replied. "He will see you and these men immediately."

Eliska turned to Gideon and translated.

"No way," Gideon said. "We need a hot bath, clean clothes, and some food first."

Eliska was about to reply when Vilém said in English, "I am afraid the count insists on seeing you immediately."

"You can tell your count to shove it up his bloody ass," Kinelly barked. "We fought our way through an army to get here, and I'm damn well going to get fed."

The servant stiffened. "You will get nothing without the count's orders."

Kinelly gritted his teeth and took a step forward.

Gideon put a hand on his arm, and said to Vilém, "I will go with Miss Dobrensky to see the count. The rest of these men will get a bath and their meal."

Vilém debated a moment, then said, "I will relay your request to the count. Please wait."

As he turned away, Eliska said to Gideon, "I apologize for this unpleasantness. But you must realize what regaining his family treasures means to Count László. Perhaps you can imagine his rage and humiliation at having his home stripped bare. Here, for example," she said, pointing to empty niches cut into the wall of the entrance hall, "rested a magnificent collection of thirteenth-century Russian icons. There, between the windows, hung a German sixteenth-century wood carving of St. Matthew. Beneath it was an ornately carved Gothic dowry chest. And these

45

were only a small portion of the collection the Hungarians seized."

Gideon studied the intense young woman for a second. "You seem very passionate about the collection yourself," he commented.

"My major responsibility as the count's secretary has been the care of his art. I have studied at museums in Paris and London. Besides, the count took me in when I was penniless and desperate. I owe him everything."

Just as she finished speaking, Vilém reappeared. He spoke to Gideon. "The count will see you and Miss Dobrensky. The others will come with me. This way, please."

The men followed him down a circular staircase that led to the lower halls. Eliska led Gideon into the castle's great hall, a long, high room of stone with wood arches spanning the upper portions of the sixty-foot ceiling. The walls of the great hall had been denuded of art, except for the large portrait of a woman over the fireplace.

"That is Countess Marian. She passed away ten years ago during childbirth. The infant died also. The tragedy wounded the count deeply. You will find him a melancholy man."

Melancholy, Gideon repeated to himself. The old-fashioned word was appropriate to these gloomy, oppressive surroundings.

The great hall opened into a secluded courtyard with a pool of Roman construction in the center. They skirted the pool, then walked down a column-supported arch bridge to a closed door.

Eliska knocked, received permission to enter, and pushed the door open.

They stepped into a wood-paneled library. Standing in front of a roaring blaze in the fireplace was Count László. He was in his late forties, a powerfully built man of medium height. He had long, black, oiled hair combed straight back from his broad forehead; thin, colorless lips; a sharp, aristocratic nose; and penetrating dark eyes.

The count stepped toward them. He said to Gideon in brusque fluent German, "You were due here two days ago."

"Unfortunately, somebody neglected to tell the Hungarian army about our schedule," Gideon said coolly.

László said, "That unfortunate circumstance means you and your men must be ready to leave immediately for Miskolc. You must attack tonight, then transfer the goods to Debrecen to be loaded onto the train before midnight tomorrow."

"We can't attack anything tonight," Gideon answered. "For one thing, we're exhausted. For another. I need today to plan the attack."

The count's eyes flashed with impatience. "I have formulated a plan. You must carry it through precisely as I say."

Eliska saw Gideon stiffen. She put her hand on the count's arm, saying, "Zsigmond, I don't—"

Count László turned and glared at her. She turned white, her hand dropped from his arm, and she stepped back. "Count László. These men have been through—"

"I did not ask your opinion," László snapped.

Gideon watched the interplay with interest. She's László's mistress, he concluded.

László turned back to Gideon. "You have an hour to prepare to leave."

"I don't need an hour," Gideon said. "We're leaving now, but we're not going to Miskolc. We were brought in because of our military expertise; instead, it seems, we're to carry out an amateur's half-baked raid. We won't have any part of it." He looked at Eliska and added, "Thank you for the rescue. Perhaps we can repay you some other time." He turned and walked toward the door.

László stared at Gideon's back for a moment. Then he called out, "Wait."

Gideon stopped and turned back toward him.

The count's lips were moving, and his expression was that of a man who had swallowed something unpleasant. Finally, he said, "Perhaps I have been presumptuous, Mr.—"

"Gideon, Scott Gideon."

"Yes, I remember. Mr. Gideon. I must tell you I have been under a great deal of stress. I think we should begin this discussion again. Please forgive my poor manners. I

47

will review the current situation for you, and you can form your own opinion of the urgency."

Gideon smiled slightly; he'd called the count's bluff by threatening to walk out on the mission. Then he said, "Fine. That's what I came here for."

"This way, please," the count said, directing Gideon to a chair by the fire. He rang for a servant, ordered coffee and cake, then sat opposite the Phoenix team leader.

"Let me review the political situation for you," Count László began. "Count Teleki, the premier, is a romantic who embraces the absurd delusion that Hungary retains her full independence and sovereignty. At the same time, he indulges in a sycophancy to the Germans that confirms the reality that Hungary is totally subservient to Hitler. Not only is the fear of German military action ever present, but hordes of brownshirted Nazi supporters stage huge mass marches through the streets whenever the government displeases them even slightly. As a result, the Germans get what they want. And that includes my wealth and that of my neighbors."

"Did they give any reason for the confiscation?"

László sneered. "Back taxes, new taxes—only the barest facade of rationality for appearance's sake. Fortunately, the Germans' greed in demanding all of the treasures works against them. There are certain government officials and army officers who do not mind the Germans' being deprived of their ill-gotten gains, if they are not directly involved and if some of the gold winds up in their pockets. That is why my private car, a freight car, and a locomotive, together with the proper transit papers to cross the border into Yugoslavia, will be waiting on a siding in Debrecen by midnight tomorrow night."

"Why Debrecen?" Gideon asked. "Wouldn't it be more direct and less dangerous to leave from Miskolc?"

Eliska answered. "From Miskolc there is only the main line to Budapest. They will block that line as a matter of course after tonight's attack."

"They'll he looking everywhere after the attack," Gideon said. "That's a good reason in itself to postpone until tomorrow night. Concealing a truck for twenty-four hours would be very difficult."

"Three trucks," Count László said. "You underestimate the volume. I have arranged for twenty men, all patriots, to travel with you to assist in loading the material after you subdue the guards. You will travel to Miskolc in the trucks, then on to Debrecen."

"That's another thing," Gideon said. "We've created such a stir that the Hungarian army is combing this area for us. Twenty-six men in three trucks traveling in a convoy would stick out like a sore thumb, not to mention the certainty of roadblocks. We've got to find another way of getting to Miskolc—we'll have to find the vehicles there."

Count László started to object. Then he exhaled and said, "I will leave such matters to you."

"What about weapons?" Gideon asked.

"We have a store of rifles and pistols."

"Machine guns or machine pistols?"

"No," Count László said.

"What about grenades?"

The count shook his head.

"Explosives?"

"Dynamite. Perhaps a case or two."

Gideon sighed. "This is going to be a longer day than I thought." He took a sip of the rich bitter coffee. "I guess it's time for me to see the diagram of the place where the art is being held. You do have a diagram?"

"Of course." László said, anger plain in his voice. "We are not fools, I assure you. You may review the plans with Pál Németh, the son of one of the nobles whose wealth has been taken. He has been trained at an Austrian military academy, and he will lead the men I am making available."

"I will be going with you also," Eliska said.

"There's no need for a woman along," Gideon said.

"A woman?" Eliska repeated angrily. "Have I not proved my courage and stamina during your rescue?"

"That's true," Gideon said. "But—"

"And I suppose you speak fluent Hungarian? And your men?"

"No."

"Few non-Hungarians do. It is a Ugrian language. The only related language in Europe is Finnish. None of the

49

local men who will be going with you know more than a few phrases."

Gideon debated. Then he shrugged in resignation. "Okay. I have no objection. You make a good case."

Eliska flashed the briefest of smiles. "I know."

Gideon got to his feet. "I've got a lot of work to do, after a little food and some sleep. One last question, Count László."

"Yes?"

"Philaix told me that after all of the art and other valuables are rescued, they will be sold in Western Europe. How can you stand the thought of losing your family heirlooms forever?"

Count László stood to face Gideon. "I share a belief held by Monsieur Philaix. Soon the "dogs of war," in the words of the English poet Shakespeare, will be unleashed upon the entire continent. My fields will be scorched, my people enslaved. My fellow nobles and I must lead the way in making sacrifices so that our beloved homeland does not fall permanently under the Nazi beasts. We must fight, with every resource we have."

He watched the expression on Gideon's face and added, "You may be assured, however, that there are limits to our sacrifices. I, too, would not trust a man who professes total selfishness. I have no intention of living as a common impoverished refugee. My friends and I have agreed to retain a portion of the proceeds from the sale in order to maintain our standard of living. I assure you that when you see the treasures, you will agree that they are more than sufficient to satisfy all parties."

"That sounds like a reasonable answer," Gideon said. "So I'll get some rest. I suppose you have people watching for Hungarian patrols?"

For the first time, László flashed a cold smile. "We do, of course. But I doubt very much that they would bother attempting a search. Within my castle there are hidden chambers and passageways that would take months, if not years, to uncover. For centuries, the László family has lived with war."

"My goal isn't to live with it," Gideon said. "My goal is to live through it."

50

6

GIDEON'S THREE HOURS' sleep had been about as satisfying as a cracker to a starving man. When Brusilov shook him awake, his eyes felt glued together, his head throbbed, and his joints seemed rusted stiff. His physical condition, together with the realization of the awesome amount of preparation that had to be done in a very limited time, made him irritable and short-tempered.

His mood wasn't improved when he met Pál Németh, a boyish-looking young man in his early twenties who had the typical ramrod-straight posture of the military cadet. Németh spread some papers on a large wooden table and began to describe the plans for the attack in German, their common tongue.

Gideon took one look and exploded. "Goddammit!" He pointed to the table. "All you have is a shitty tourist map. I suppose you were thinking of waltzing in with picnic baskets under our arms, stuffing in the art, and walking back out."

Nemeth stiffened. "But the Chapel of St. István is a museum."

Kinelly reared. "We're attacking a church?"

Gideon shot a glance at him and said sardonically, "Your religious faith is touching, Oscar." He looked back at Németh. "Why in the hell would they keep the stuff there?"

"The building has not been used for religious services for centuries, since the Turkish occupation. Instead, its

51

numerous catacombs have been used as a cataloguing warehouse for various state museums. The main floor has been partially restored, and is used for small exhibitions open to the public. I have visited the chapel two or three times. The guards were all old men, retired police and soldiers. They should present little problem."

Gideon stared at the young man in disbelief. "You think they've decided to store millions of dollars' worth of art and gold and silver, stuff that Hitler's drooling over, in this chapel, and they let the same old men guard it? I've never heard anything so idiotic."

Németh blanched. Beginning to tremble, he turned and started for the door.

Immediately Gideon regretted his harshness. In the military academy, he thought, this kid probably had spent his time learning close-order drill and memorizing the details of Napoleon's campaigns. That was about as useful as the modern veterinarian studying the physiology of dinosaurs. For the type of war he was going to have to fight in the future, he would have been better off getting his education in the hills with smugglers and bandits.

"Hold it," Gideon called out.

Németh stopped near the door.

"I didn't mean to take it out on you," Gideon said. "I know you were doing what the count told you to do. Come on back and let me explain something to you."

Németh debated. "I was only trying to do my best," he said.

Gideon clapped him on the shoulder. "I have a very important job for you. If we're going to get into the chapel without getting killed, have the time to load the trucks, and get them a hundred kilometers to Debrecen, we're going to need one hell of a plan. And planning means up-to-date intelligence."

"You mean we have to know current security arrangements?"

"And a lot more." Gideon said. "I don't want to trust to luck that we can take the chapel quietly enough not to attract attention. The best way to guard against interruption is to create a hell of a ruckus someplace else."

"You mean a diversionary attack?"

"Or two," Gideon said. "That will be the job of you and your men. How were you planning to get your men to Miskolc?"

"Most of them are already there, or on their way. We were operating under the assumption that the attack would take place tonight. I and my second-in-command were to travel with you in the moving vans. We have obtained papers for the shipment of household goods from here to Budapest."

Gideon said, "I think one van on the road with three men in it won't attract too much attention. Joel," he said, turning to the Dutchman.

"Yes?"

"I want you to go with Németh to Miskolc. You've got to leave right away. Scout this chapel as thoroughly as you can. And I want you to pick out targets for two diversionary attacks."

"What are we looking for?" In'Hout asked.

"Factories, or railroad shipping yards. We don't want a place that's heavily fortified, or a place where we'd risk heavy civilian casualties. But we want a target important enought to get army units mobilized."

"We'll do it," In'Hout said.

Gideon turned to Németh. "We need a spot to meet. Late afternoon tomorrow. In case we get held up, it should be someplace you two can sit without attracting attention."

Németh thought. "I know a café, the Central, in the southern part of the city. A lot of students go there. We should pass unnoticed."

"Tell me how to find it," Gideon said.

"That will not be necessary," Eliska said. "I know that café. I can lead you there."

"Good," Gideon said. "We'll try to be there by five." He looked at In'Hout. "I'm sending you because of your fluent German. Remember, Germans are VIPs in Hungary now. That may help you bluff your way out of a tight spot. You'll be traveling in one of the moving vans, so you may meet a roadblock."

In'Hout nodded. As he and Pál Németh left the room, Gideon said, "Ian, Charvey, Kinelly, I've got an idea how you'll travel." He asked Eliska, "Are there any monasteries in this area?"

"Yes, of course. Three within twenty kilometers."

"I got an idea from the mention of the chapel. We have to find a way to transport our weapons and equipment. We'll pack them in crates labeled as if they contained fragile icons being shipped to this chapel. You three will dress as monks to go along."

"How will we travel?" Ian asked.

"Eliska, where is the nearest rail line?"

"Užgorod. From there, the Magyar Államvasutak, the Royal Hungarian State Railways, has a major direct line to Miskolc."

"You men will ride the train," Gideon said. "When you get to Miskolc, you'll locate a large transport company, ostensibly arranging for moving the icons to the Chapel of St. István. You want a place that has the kind of large vans we'll need later. Have the crates picked up and stored at the transport company. We'll pay a little unauthorized visit later to pick them up."

"How are we going to do this?" Charvey asked. "None of us speaks Hungarian."

"We need someone to go along who does," Gideon said. He noticed Eliska about to speak, then added, "No, not you. You're traveling with Brusilov and me. We need someone else who speaks Hungarian."

Eliska frowned. "That might be difficult. Other than Vilém, there is no—"

"Vilém is perfect," Gideon said.

"That's impossible." Eliska protested. "He is the count's personal servant. Count László depends on him. He would never permit him to go with you."

"If he wants his treasure back, he'll agree," Gideon snapped. "If he doesn't, then you let me know right now and I'll get some more sleep."

Eliska's face was red. "You are a very rude man," she said.

Gideon smiled. "Thank you. Now scoot off and talk to the count."

He watched her leave the room. Then he turned to

Charvey and said, "Marcel, I've got a special job for you. You know railroads?"

"Am I not secretary of the International Federation of Transport Workers? Was I not a wiper on the Paris-Lyon *rapide* practically before I could walk?"

"While you're on this trip, I want you to pick up schedules and study the rail routes as thoroughly as you can. And check out the switching procedures, communication systems, and anything else you notice."

Charvey asked, "You are anticipating problems on the train in Debrecen?"

"Who knows?" Gideon said. "Preparation can't hurt."

"*D'accord*," Charvey said.

"So you three see about building crates. And have someone go out to fetch clerical outfits for you. Kinelly, you're going to have to do something about that hair."

The Irishman sat bolt upright. "What do you mean?"

"I haven't seen many red-headed monks in this part of Europe. You have to dye your hair."

"Over my dead bloody body," Kinelly retorted.

Brusilov got to his feet. He towered over Kinelly. "Maybe you would like a haircut like mine," he said, running his hand over his bald pate.

"Get away from me, you big oaf," Kinelly snapped, although he could not keep a small smile from his lips.

The other men were laughing. Gideon said with a smile, "Think about it, Kinelly. Dye your hair, or I appoint Brusilov the official Phoenix barber."

"Bloody Russian," Kinelly muttered.

Gideon said to Brusilov, "Come with me. It's time to check the weapons."

A servant directed them through a long gallery, which ran the length of the building's side that overlooked the valley. Sunlight filtering through the windows spread in golden patterns across the opposing wall, illuminating the bare whiter expanses where paintings had hung.

Eliska met them in the room. She pointed to an empty space. "A tavern scene by Adriaen Brouwer hung there," she said. "Next to it was Rembrandt's *Music Lesson*, then a Verspronck and a Gerard Ter Borch. Over on the far wall was Teniers' *Soldiers at an Inn*."

55

The animation in the young woman's voice and face struck a chord in Gideon. He was reminded again that while he and the other team members were professional soldiers carrying out a military operation. Eliska, László, and the others were involved in an intensely emotional quest. Of course, Gideon couldn't let their feelings influence his professional judgment. But he must try to be less impatient with them for the mission to succeed.

That reminder was fresh in his mind when Eliska escorted him into another chamber. Sitting in the middle of the floor was a pile of rifles and pistols of unfathomable vintage and manufacture. What a prize collection, Gideon thought. That junk was worthy of a museum display, but the notion of firing any of it made him cringe.

He kept the disappointment from creeping into his voice. He asked Eliska, "What about dynamite?"

"I'll have the case brought in."

A few minutes later, a servant came in carrying a crate, which he set down roughly on the floor. The top of the crate had been opened previously, so Gideon had no trouble prying up a slat and sliding his hand inside. He felt the packing straw and, below that, the sticks. They were moist.

He rose, and when he spoke there was urgency in his voice. "How old is that stuff?"

The servant shrugged. "It has always been here."

"Well, it's sweating. Open that crate and stuff it full of ice at once. And I mean at once. Then put it carefully into a larger container and fill that with ice. Sweaty dynamite could go off just sitting there."

The servant paled, then hurried off to get ice.

Gideon watched him go, his lips tight.

"What do you think?" Brusilov asked.

"This stuff's useless for close combat."

"What I would give for that MP40 I left in the cave," Brusilov said.

"What I'd give for a half-dozen of them," Gideon said. He asked Eliska, "Do you have shotguns?"

"The men who watch the herds use them. They—"

"Get me six. Double-barreled if possible. Avrahm,

56

you'll cut down the barrels. That'll give us plenty of punch for the assault on the chapel."

Brusilov nodded. Eliska started out of the room, but Gideon stopped her. "Not so fast." he said. "I'm going to give you a shopping list."

"What do you mean?"

"I mean that since we don't have any grenades or dynamite or other explosives, we're going to have to improvise. Do you have black powder?"

"Yes," Eliska said.

"Good. I need a couple kegs. Then I need a quantity of iron pipe, say three inches in diameter. A pipe cutter— you can use that to saw off the shotguns, Avrahm. And pipe caps. And a drill. And—"

"Please," Eliska said. "I'm not going to remember this. Come with me. We'll gather some servants to help."

"I can use your help, too," Gideon said. "You're about to become a munitions specialist."

Later that afternoon, Gideon had set up an isolated lower chamber of the castle as a makeshift laboratory. He held up an eight-inch length of pipe with both ends threaded. He said to Eliska, "We'll put a pipe cap on one end of these and fill them with black powder. The tough part is getting these pipe grenades to go off. That means making fuse cord and detonators."

"How do we do that?" Eliska asked.

"You'll do the fuse cord. That's easier. Take some black powder and grind it fine. Add a little water to make a paste. Then braid three strands of soft cotton string together and rub the paste into it. After it dries, cut some into four-inch lengths for the grenades—that'll give us about a five-second delay. The rest of the cord you can leave in two- or three-foot lengths."

Eliska nodded, then set to work.

Gideon turned to Brusilov. "Now for the detonators. You have the used rifle cartridges?"

"Dozens."

"Good. Take a nail and scrape out the fired primer. Then drill a hole in the primer pocket large enough to receive the fuse cord Eliska is preparing. When her cord dries, tie a knot in the end of a four-inch length and pass it through the hole from the inside. That'll prevent the fuse from falling out."

"What about the explosive?"

"That I've got to make," Gideon said.

He needed both a primary explosive and a booster for the detonator. If he'd had some plastic explosive, he could have solved the problem by leaching from it RDX, which would serve both functions. Then again, if he'd had plastic explosive, he probably would have had military blasting caps and he wouldn't have to go through this whole damn process.

After questioning Vilém and the manager of László's estates, he'd found he didn't have the right materials to make TACC, DDNP, or mercury fulminate as the primary explosive. Then he came across a quantity of army-issue heat tablets that had found their way into the hands of the men who stayed out all night with the flocks. The tablets, he knew, contained hexamethylenetetramine, the primary ingredient in HMTD, an explosive that would work fine.

He began by pouring a quantity of hair bleach into a large container. In three portions, he dissolved the crushed heat tablets into the hair bleach. He placed the container in a pan of cold water and let it sit.

After the mixture was chilled, he dissolved crushed citric acid into it. Then he poured the liquid into a large, flat baking pan. Soon solid particles of HMTD would form at the bottom of the pan. When the precipitation was complete, he'd filter the mixture through cheesecloth. As soon as the solid particles dried, they'd be ready to use.

While he waited for the HMTD to precipitate, he started making the booster. The source of the main ingredient for the booster made him smile. Common aspirin was normally used to cure headaches. He was going to make from it picric acid, which would help give a giant headache to the Hungarian army.

He crushed a quantity of aspirin in a beaker. He added a little water to make a paste, then poured in alcohol. He filtered the solution through cheesecloth, discarded the solid material, then placed the filtered liquid in a dish sitting in a pan of hot water.

Soon the liquid evaporated, leaving a fine white powder. He poured the powder into sulfuric acid he'd gotten from old batteries. The solution turned orange-yellow. He added saltpeter. The solution turned red, then started to change back to orange-yellow again.

Brusilov, who had finished preparing the detonator cases, was watching with rapt attention. He said, "I did not know you were a sorcerer."

Gideon smiled. "It's not sorcery. Just simple chemistry. I knew this stuff would come in handy someday."

"What happens next?"

"I add some cold water, mix, then pour the liquid through cheesecloth. Light-yellow crystals of picric acid will be filtered out. When they and the HMTD dry, we'll pack the cartridges you made and finish assembling the pipe grenades. In the meantime, we'll work on another little surprise for the Hungarians."

"What's that?" Brusilov asked.

"We're going to make fudge."

"Do not kid me."

"Watch," Gideon said. He heated water over a low flame in a large pot. Then he poured in saltpeter and, to Brusilov's amazement, a large quantity of sugar.

Just before the liquid started to boil, Gideon added rust that he scraped off some old metal that had been sitting around.

Like a fussy cook, Gideon stirred the liquid until it was reduced to about one quarter of its initial volume. The material reached the consistency of fudge.

"Witchcraft, I still maintain," Brusilov said.

"I hope this is a good batch," Gideon said. "Since Pál Németh and his men won't have any automatic weapons, I want to beef up their firepower."

"How will fudge do that?"

"I'll show you. Hand me one of those lengths of half-inch-thick board I had you cut."

Brusilov handed him a one-foot-square piece of lumber.

Gideon took a scoop of the "fudge" and covered one

side of the board. From a small keg he took a handful of small nails and scattered them on top of the sticky goo. He patted them down, then tied around the board a substantial length of the fuse cord Eliska had prepared.

When he was done, Brusilov said, "I still do not understand."

"All Németh has to do to keep a large number of troops tied down is to prop up these boards with the nail side toward the enemy. When the fuse is burned down, it will ignite the 'fudge,' which is an excellent small-arms propellant. Each of those sixty or seventy nails will fly off like shrapnel."

"My God!" Brusilov exclaimed. He picked up one of the nails, rotating it in his huge hand. "That will make a awful wound."

"That's the idea." Gideon said. "Now, you can help me make them. We've got to get these and the pipe grenades finished and packed so Ian, Charvey, and Kinelly can leave this evening."

"How are we going to Miskolc?" Brusilov asked.

"In style, my friend," Gideon said. "Even though we destroyed his favorite limousine, the count has graciously permitted us to take another car. You will be the chauffeur. Eliska and I will ride in the back—an aristocrat and his wife."

"What a thought," Brusilov said, "to be married to that one. Better I should marry a she-wolf."

"A she-wolf may be what you need," Gideon answered, "when your honeymoon involves fighting through the entire Hungarian army."

7

A FRIGID RAIN was falling as they started off the next morning. Brusilov, jammed uncomfortably into an altered but still ill-fitting chauffeur's uniform, grunted as he steered the Mercedes down the treacherous muddy road leading from the castle to the valley.

Gideon and Eliska sat in silence in the rear. The atmosphere was strained after a shouting match with László. Just before they set off, the count demanded a full description of Gideon's plans for his approval. Gideon, who had managed only two more hours' sleep, brusquely told him it was standard procedure for the fewest possible people to know the entire plan. László had been furious.

Once again, he'd turned on Eliska in his wrath. Gideon had found out from the estate manager that she was indeed his mistress. For the life of him, Gideon couldn't understand why a woman as beautiful and intelligent as she would put up with a man like László, even with his heritage and title. He was tempted to ask her, but he decided not to risk that confrontation.

They reached the village of Petres, but the road did not improve. It wound around pinnacles, plunged into canyons, and coiled up along the ledges of deep ravines. Gideon tried to doze, but lurching awake to see the car had less than a foot of clearance to the edge of the precipice permanently opened his eyes.

Two hours later, when they reached the highway to Užgorod, Brusilov pulled wearily over to the side of the road to let Gideon spell him at the wheel. Thirty kilometers down the road, they reached Užgorod, which was in sight of the German-controlled "independent" Slovakia. Eliska directed them onto a shortcut that avoided the border by cutting south-southwest across the strip of South Slovakia which had been ceded to Hungary as its prize in the 1938 "Vienna Award" with Hitler.

The shortcut was paved, but it, too, writhed and slithered through the mountains like an agonized snake. Gideon's face grew taut with exertion as the Mercedes, its engine howling, struggled up and down the steep slopes.

Shortly after noon, they arrived at Král and the adjacent Sátoraljaújhely, which had once been the twin frontier towns between Czechoslovakia and Hungary. Brusilov once again resumed driving, in case they were stopped, but the old border posts were closed, their iron gates standing open and mud-splashed by traffic.

"The worst is over," Eliska said. "The road from here to Miskolc is quite good."

"Up to now it's been murder," Gideon said.

"We could have gone instead by way of Mukačevo and the old border town of Cop. It would have been easier driving, but we would have run a greater risk of patrols."

"We should be beyond the area where they're searching for us specifically," Gideon said. "And that's a relief."

He leaned back against the seat, enjoying the smoother ride. He became conscious that Eliska was staring at him before she spoke.

"May I ask you something?" she said.

"Sure."

"I am curious. You have taken such risks to get here. I don't understand why. Your country is not at war."

"No," Gideon said. "But America should be. The U.S. should have gotten together with Britain and France two years ago and stopped Hitler in his tracks. Now Germany is so strong he's likely to take all of Europe."

Eliska pondered the reply. Then she asked, "Is that your only reason? You don't seem to me like a political man."

"You don't have to be political to believe strongly in

what's right and wrong. But you're correct—that wasn't the only reason I joined Phoenix."

"Was it—"

"It wasn't money," Gideon said.

"I wasn't going to ask that."

"Most people do," Gideon said. "But I'm not a mercenary, no more than any soldier. What I am is a man who believes most people are so afraid of dying that they're already half dead. All my life, the more risks I've taken, the more alive I felt. I get pleasure from doing what other men can't and don't dare to do. And there's no place like war to prove a man's worth. Rank, wealth, power—they don't mean a bloody thing."

The reference to Count László was obvious. Gideon expected Eliska to retort. Instead, she reddened, looking down at her hands. Then she leaned back, staring silently out the window at the passing countryside.

Traffic was sparse for the next hour. But shortly after they passed the intersection with the highway that led from Nyíregyháza and Miskolc, traffic in front of them began to slow. Soon they were moving at an infuriating creep.

"Construction, perhaps?" Eliska asked hopefully.

"I wish it were," Gideon said, glimpsing a lamplight flashing on a barricade. "It's a roadblock."

As they got closer, they could see Hungarian soldiers in rain slickers and hats standing around a trestle blockade and along the shoulders of the road. A khaki-colored Skoda sedan was parked almost flanking their car, its windows steamed opaque except for the driver's, which was rolled down. Silhouettes were visible of two other men in the car, and it wasn't hard to guess that the one sitting in the rear was the one in charge.

Gideon turned to Eliska. "Are you ready?" he asked.

She nodded. Then she opened the door and headed straight for three soldiers who were coming to inspect the car. Smiling, she locked arms with one of the soldiers and continued toward the staff car. A moment later she was talking with the man in back, her hand toying with the buttons of his tunic.

Gideon and Brusilov watched in amazement as Eliska

63

transformed herself into a flirting coquette. The charade seemed to be working perfectly.

Then they were startled by rapping on the driver's window. A fourth soldier stood there, gesturing and shouting at Brusilov, who couldn't understand a word. As the soldier rapped again, Brusilov shot a worried glance back at Gideon.

Gideon acted quickly. He grabbed a flask of brandy, swished the liquid around in his mouth, then swallowed. At the same time, he opened the door of the limousine and got out.

The soldier turned to look at him. Gideon flashed him a drunken smile, staggered a couple steps, then stopped. In the middle of the road, he unbuttoned his fly and began to urinate.

He heard an angry shout from behind him. A soldier's hand was on his shoulder. Gideon spun, still pissing. The urine soaked the soldier's trouser leg.

He jumped back, his face a mask of fury. He looked for an instant as if he were going to take a swing at Gideon. Then he pivoted and started to storm off toward the officer's car.

The officer, holding Eliska's right hand between his two, was smiling and laughing as he escorted her back to her car. The angry soldier approached and started gesturing, but the officer flashed him a glare and waved him off.

Gideon was back in the car by the time the officer opened the door for Eliska. He bowed, kissing her hand. Then the door closed and Brusilov accelerated away from the roadblock.

They contained themselves until they were out of sight. Then they broke out, roaring with laughter.

"That soldier!" Brusilov exclaimed. "The look on his face when you pissed on him!"

"Who says Phoenix does not get its revenge?" Gideon said. "For some reason, the story about the Hungarian cavalryman pissing on Kinelly leaped into my mind."

Eliska was laughing so hard tears were coming to her eyes. "That officer, such a pushover," she said. "He was so full of understanding for the poor young girl forced to live in the mountains with her drunken lout of a husband.

He was so sympathetic that I'd finally reached my limit and demanded my husband take me to my mother's in Miskolc for a visit. And he was so anxious to get my mother's address for his next leave."

"You were perfect," Gideon said with admiration. "And it's good to see you laugh."

Eliska was dabbing at her eyes with a handkerchief when she spoke. "I used to laugh all of the time," she said. "My home was a happy one. Since I lost everything and everyone dear to me, there has been little reason to laugh."

"The Castle László is not a very happy place, it seems to me," Gideon said.

"The count saved my life." Eliska said. "I owe him so much."

"He's a widower," Gideon said. "At least he could marry you."

"I would not expect him to make that sacrifice," Eliska said. "The next Countess László must be a woman of wealth and rank. Perhaps he will find her in France or England. Until then, he bears the weight of the struggle against Fascism. I am privileged to serve him."

All traces of laughter were gone, and the familiar serious look had returned to Eliska's face. Gideon turned away, and they continued down the highway in silence.

When they finally arrived at Miskolc, a city of 200,000 people clustered at the foot of the Bükk Mountains, it was four o'clock in the afternoon. While they were crossing the Sajó River into the city, the rain unexpectedly stopped, the clouds folding back and the sun appearing for the first time that day. A fine mist rose from the streets under the pallid yet welcome sunlight, the brick and copper pavements turning to deeper, richer shades of brown, tan, and umber.

"We've got an hour until we meet Németh and In'Hout," Gideon said, "I'd like to drive around to get an idea of the layout of the city."

"I lived here for two years," Eliska said, "studying the famous Scythian ruins. I can direct you."

As they moved down the main thoroughfares, Eliska pointed out the law school, the restored fifteenth-century cathedral, and, in the heart of the city, Avas Hill with its honeycomb of wine cellars.

Gideon became interested in watching the citizenry. As the hour moved on, people started appearing in greater numbers. At first Gideon was reminded of the traditional Spanish promenade, when everyone would go for a stroll as the sun was going down. But Gideon got the sense that the people of Miskolc weren't strolling for a breath of fresh air. Rather, they were milling, as if expecting something to happen. And though the women were all in normal winter clothing, he saw mixed with the fedoras and overcoats of the men an increasing number of uniforms.

The uniformed men weren't police or army; they were obviously civilians. Their uniforms were paramilitary: stiffly pressed brown shirts and pants, brilliantly polished boots, Sam Browne belts, and jaunty caps perched on their close-cropped heads.

"This isn't usual, is it?" Gideon asked. "Is this a holiday?"

"I don't know," Eliska said. "But those men in uniform are the members of the group Count László mentioned."

"The brownshirts," Brusilov said with disgust. "They remind me of Germany, before the war."

"Here they belong to a party called the Arrow Front," Eliska said. "Their power and influence grow daily."

"I can guess what they preach," Gideon said. He looked at his watch, then added, "It's almost five, and I've seen enough. Let's find that café."

The drive through heavy traffic to the drab suburb on the outskirts of Miskolc took twenty minutes. Eliska directed Brusilov to park the Mercedes near a corner building with a sign over it reading *Étterem Arany*. The café they entered was filled with men in working clothes, with a few in cheap suits. By the bar was a cluster of noisy brownshirts, and the radio behind them was blaring martial music. Gideon felt the hair on the back of his neck rise.

Eliska whispered, "This place has changed since I was here last."

"It's too late now," Gideon said. "We'll have to make

the best of it, even though we stand out like sore thumbs."

Brusilov nudged Gideon. "Over in the far corner."

Gideon saw Németh and In'Hout nursing beers at a round table. He led the way through the crowd and sat down.

A waiter approached before they had a chance to do more than exchange greetings. Eliska ordered the same meal for them all: pork cooked with onions, peppers, garlic and hot *feferoni* paprika; and wine.

When the waiter moved off, Gideon whispered to Németh, "were you successful?"

"I have drawn plans of the approach to the chapel," he replied, "The museum itself was closed. Let me show—"

Gideon put a hand on his arm. "Not here. I'll go over them in detail with Joel later. What about the other targets?"

"It was difficult moving around today. Today is March sixteenth, the first anniversary of that black day when Germany dissolved Czechoslovakia and let the Magyars seize my homeland. The government has declared today Hungarian-German Solidarity Day. There were noontime speeches and a rally for schoolchildren, and a parade is scheduled for tonight."

"So," Gideon said, "that explains what's going on." He thought for a moment, then added, "I think it's a break for us. The parade will concentrate the police and army units. We're less likely to run into a random patrol."

"I hope that is true," Németh said. His face was drawn and pale, and Gideon could see that the tension of the day was telling on him. He hoped to hell the young man wouldn't collapse; his role in the mission was vital.

"Did you pick targets?" Gideon asked.

"We have two. A central mail-sorting facility and a textile plant. The first is directly west of the city, the second farther south, along the main rail line to Budapest."

Gideon looked at In'Hout. "You're satisfied with these, Joel?"

In'Hout nodded. He was about to speak, but then he saw the waiter approach with the food.

Brusilov took a bite of the highly spiced mixture, then

67

waved his hand back and forth in front of his mouth. "If we are attacked," he said, "all we have to do is breathe on them."

Suddenly, the café fell hushed. Gideon, who was questioning Németh about his plans, let his voice trail off.

A short fanfare blasted over the radio. It was followed by a voice that sounded metallic, as if the man were speaking through a filter mike.

"Ferenc Szalási," Eliska whispered. "The leader of the brownshirts."

"What's he saying?" Gideon asked.

She translated the highlights as Szalási spoke: "Hungary cannot falter in her resolve to rectify the injustices inflicted upon her by the infamous Treaty of Trianon . . . Our appeals to Greater Germany have resulted in the return of the Carpatho-Ukraine and Southern Slovakia, and we can count on the Third Reich to aid our regaining of the Bác-Kiskun and all other sovereign regions. . . . But we can not sit idle while the New Europe is being forged. . . . If we are to be a nation no longer puny, divided, helpless, and shamed, we must be willing to shed blood as partners, destroying the forces of Communism and Zionism that stand in our way."

The men at the bar and the surrounding tables listened with eyes shining, lips parted in proud, acquiescent smiles. When Ferenc Szalási ceased speaking, they enthusiastically applauded.

Gideon and the others sat still. In'Hout, whose shins bore permanent scars from his torture by German brownshirts in Berlin, was deathly pale as he fought for control.

Their passivity brought them to the notice of other patrons. They saw scowls, and whispered remarks. Someone pointed them out to the loudest of the brownshirts standing at the bar, a short, stocky man with oily black hair and a thick mustache. The man came swaggering over to their table.

Gideon could see In'Hout tense even more. "Stay calm," he whispered.

The man came up and began haranguing them in Hungarian. They didn't need Eliska to translate to figure out that he was berating them for not joining in the applause.

Then the brownshirt noticed In'Hout. He glanced down and saw that In'Hout hadn't touched the pork on his plate. A look of suspicion came onto his face.

The whole café was watching them now, some of the brownshirts gathering to stand behind their spokesman.

In'Hout was looking down at the table. The man reached out, grabbed his chin, and pulled his head up to get a better look at his features. "Do we have a Jew here?" he asked loudly.

Gideon could see that In'Hout was a hair's-breadth away from attacking. It was time to act. He leaped to his feet, stamped his foot on the floor, and began shouting in German, "How dare you? How dare you touch a citizen of the Third Reich? Are Hungarians such brutes they refuse to honor this day of friendship?"

The brownshirts didn't understand what he was saying, but the fluent German set them back a bit.

Eliska immediately took up on Gideon's cue. "You have insulted Herr Rheinhardt," she cried in Hungarian.

Gideon turned and barked at her in German.

Eliska rose. "He demands that the police be summoned. He demands an investigation of how German citizens are treated in Hungary."

The stocky man with the mustache continued to stare at them suspiciously. But the proprietor of the place came rushing up with an unctuous look on his face. "No police," he said. "No need. This is all a misunderstanding."

Gideon continued to survey the crowd with a haughty look in his eye. Then he gestured to the others and started to make his way through the crowd.

The brownshirt only grudgingly made room to let them by. The tension in the air was thick. As In'Hout pushed his way past, the brownshirt leaned forward and hissed, "Filthy Jew!"

In'Hout stopped. His hand started to rise. Then Brusilov grabbed him and pushed him ahead. The brownshirt took a step forward, but the Russian shot him a fierce glare. He halted.

They reached the sidewalk and hurried to the Mercedes. When they got inside, Gideon said, "Avrahm, get the hell out of here quick."

69

In'Hout was grim and trembling. "I wanted to kill him," he said.

"You'll get your chance to pay them back in a couple hours. That wasn't the time or place. You know that?"

In'Hout nodded.

Gideon turned to Németh. "We're heading to the train station to meet Charvey, Kinelly, and Ian. They'll lead us to the crates of weapons and explosives at the moving company. We'll take the vehicles we need and get rolling." He looked at his watch. "It's quarter to six now. At seven, we'll provide some fireworks for that Nazi celebration."

8

THE SETUP WAS bad enough. Their luck was worse.

The Chapel of St. István was four kilometers outside of the Miskolc city limits, just off the same main highway south they'd have to take to reach the cutoff to Debrecen. From that highway an access road ran half a kilometer, dipped under a railroad trestle, then rose another half kilometer to the chapel, built on top of a rounded knoll overlooking the Sajó River.

The land from the chapel to the main highway, on either side of the access road, was a vast acreage of cropped meadowland.

"It looks like a park," In'Hout had said, describing it to Gideon.

"It is a park," Eliska had explained. "It's a popular area for outings in warm weather."

As Gideon had studied the diagram, he had grimaced. There was too much open ground and no way out other than the road. If something went wrong, that road could easily be blocked and they'd have to flee over open land without cover.

As it turned out, they didn't have time to worry about getting out. Wooden barricades manned by a half-dozen soldiers had been set up at the junction with the main highway where they planned to exit.

Gideon was in the lead of their mini-caravan, driving the moving van in which Németh and In'Hout had traveled to Miskolc. It was a Czech-built Tatra, a six-and-a-half-ton, with six-wheel chassis and a twenty-five-foot-long body with latching double doors side and rear. Behind him, Brusilov and Charvey drove two smaller moving vans the Phoenix team had "liberated" from the transport company lot. Eliska brought up the rear in the Mercedes.

The huge Tatra had weak brakes and a loose front end, and Gideon was concentrating so hard keeping it on the highway that he didn't notice the roadblock until the last minute. After a split second of indecision, he kept his foot on the accelerator and breezed past the exit to the access road without slowing. It was nearly a kilometer before he found a spot to pull off to the side of the road.

Gideon jumped out of the cab. In'Hout reached him first. "That checkpoint was not there this afternoon," he said.

"Did you see those uniforms?" Brusilov asked. "Those are not regular army soldiers. Those black felt hats with cockerel feather plumes are the badge of the elite Royal Hungarian Gendarmerie."

"Great," Gideon grunted.

"Can we take them?" Charvey asked.

Gideon shook his head. "Not on the main highway. It'll take at least an hour to load the trucks. With the mess we'd make, we wouldn't get fifteen minutes before someone happened by and reported it."

"What about the diversionary attacks?" Ian asked. "Will that draw them away?"

"We can't wait to find out," Gideon said. "Remember, we have a train to catch." He turned to Charvey. "You're our best knife man, Marcel. Let's you and I go take a look."

They set off at a trot along the side of the road until they could just make out the blockade at the entrance to the access road. Keeping low to the ground, they cut through a roadside ditch to the broad meadow. They were grateful for the failing light—they had changed into their black pants and black sweaters with the small Phoenix emblem, so they were hard to spot against the dark ground.

They cut on an angle toward the access road. When

they neared the railroad trestle, the land dipped out of sight of the roadblock, and they ran under the tracks and up the small knoll on the other side.

Gideon dropped to the ground. Ahead, the road ran through large rock cairns flanking a pair of heart-shaped gates. The gates were shut and appeared to be locked. Shrubbery and small trees grew thickly around the cairns, but not quite thickly enough to shroud the sentry booth that stood just on the other side of the gates, or the two uniformed men silhouetted by the light within.

Beyond the gates, the road branched as it continued toward the chapel. The right fork disappeared out of view—Gideon remembered from In'Hout's briefing that it led to a courtyard fronting the main entrance. The left fork went to a loading dock abutting the rear warehouse.

From their position, they couldn't see what, if anything, was in the loading area. The rest of the chapel, however, rose in stark outline against the now dusky sky. It was medieval, all stone and tall grated windows—some of which were lit—and massive inset doors behind which would be dozens of interlocking rooms. There were spires and porticoes and a graceful belfry on the roof.

Gideon whispered to Charvey, "We have to get closer." The Frenchman nodded.

Gideon led the way, sprinting hunched through the only grove of trees growing in proximity to the fence. Hunkering down at the other end of the grove, they studied the wide stretch of open field between them and the fence, then the fence and its flanking shrubbery. The fence was low, more decorative than defensive. But the bushes were scraggly and meager, offering scant concealment, though they gradually became thicker as they neared the sentry booth a hundred yards to the left.

Flattened on their bellies, Gideon and Charvey began to wriggle toward the fence. It was an agonizingly slow crawl on their elbows and knees, the sodden grass and earth soaking their clothes to the skin. The chilly dampness made Gideon's old buttock wound begin to ache, the wound he had gotten sneaking the same way across a field in the Spanish Civil War. The memory of it, and the similarities to his present predicament, were like

73

acid eating into his gut. He could feel the sweat beading his forehead as he forced himself to worm forward the remaining feet. He sagged, breathless, when his hand brushed the fence.

From where he was, he could see the loading area. Floodlamps cast beams down the building's gutter line, illuminating an expanse of pavement and platform dock that fronted a series of closed garage doors. Parked in a row along the middle of the dock were three trucks—standard Mercedes three-tonners, by their look, with canvas-topped beds and no markings on them, military or otherwise. On the far right side of the dock was a regular door, and standing beside it was another guard, smoking a cigarette.

The sight of the trucks gladdened Gideon's heart. He had finally hit a stroke of luck, not having to figure out a way to get the huge Tatra and the other two vans into the compound past the roadblock. All he had to do was figure a way to get out.

He watched for a few moments, weighing his next move. They could either make their way back to the road to get the rest of the team or take the gate sentries out now. His aching butt made up Gideon's mind for him—he'd rather risk challenging the sentries than make his torturous way back over open ground.

He motioned to Charvey, who nodded his understanding. Scaling the fence was easy, a quick scramble putting them up and over. They eased closer to the booth, slithering from shrub to shrub, continually wary of making a noise that would attract a sentry. They reached the last clump of brush without incident.

Now they could hear muffled voices within the booth, droning in desultory tones. That meant the sentries were bored, a good sign.

Gideon spotted a rusty junction box on the rear wall of the booth, with two cables running up to the roof and across to a high pole made from a debarked tree trunk. Craning his head, he saw the cables were spliced into a line of wires strung on other poles running across the park. Those would be the main electrical and telephone connections from the chapel to Miskolc, he thought. He

74

would have risked inching in and cutting the booth's phone line, if he'd known which one it was. Slice the wrong cable, and he'd probably electrocute himself, at the same time causing a blackout that would put the guards on instant alert.

Gideon turned his attention back to the problem of these sentries. He whispered to Charvey, who slid on his belly from the brush and eased alongside the booth.

Gideon waited until he was in place. Then he let out a high-pitched yip.

The conversation in the booth stopped. He could see a guard's face at the window.

Gideon yipped again, louder.

The guard cursed. He stepped out of the booth toward the gate, while the other guard watched from the doorway.

Charvey was on the first sentry. One meaty hand clutched his throat in a half stranglehold as the sentry was wrenched off balance. Then the knife descended with a moist thunk, plunging into the heart.

Gideon lunged forward. The other sentry had stepped back inside the booth, and he had the phone in his hand when Gideon dragged him out of the booth. The sentry struggled hard, one hand holding the telephone while its cord stretched taut behind him like a rubber band. Gideon, forsaking his knife, used the butt of his Luger to knock him out with a swift blow to the skull.

Gideon dove into the booth and yanked the phone cord from the wall. Then he stood, motionless, waiting for a sign that the commotion had been noticed or that a phone connection had been made.

The seconds ticked by with agonizing slowness. Finally, Gideon breathed a sigh of relief. "So far, so good," he said to Charvey.

"What now?" Charvey asked.

Gideon glanced around until he spotted the key to the gates hanging on a nail by the door. He removed it, then said, "I'm going out the gates and back to the team. You relock them, then get the bodies out of the way. If somebody comes up, you'll have to use your judgment."

Charvey nodded, his face grim. "Hurry back," he said.

Compared to the crawl to the gates, the run back down the road, underneath the trestle, then across the field seemed very short. When he reached the parked trucks, the team members gathered around anxiously.

"We thought you had run into trouble," Brusilov said.

Gideon shook his head as he caught his breath. He drank in a couple gulps of oxygen, then explained, "We took the sentries at the gate out. Charvey is there waiting for us."

"How do we get through that roadblock?" Ian asked.

"We don't." Gideon replied. "I'll explain later." He turned to In'Hout. "Joel, you've got to take the Mercedes and get to Németh as fast as you can. That second attack on the textile factory isn't going to do us any good if we're up to our asses here. Get him and his men back here as fast as you can."

In'Hout's eyes flashed with anger. "But—"

Gideon put a hand on his arm. "I know you want to make up for this afternoon. And I know you don't want to have to make your way through any more brownshirts. But you're the only one who knows exactly where he is."

"You'll be short a gun," In'Hout said.

"No, you won't," Eliska said, stepping forward. She had changed into clothing similar to that worn by the Phoenix team. "I'll take the shotgun."

Gideon looked at her. "All right." He turned back to In'Hout. "We don't have time to waste."

In'Hout's lips were tight. Then he said, "I'll do it."

Pál Németh lay on his belly on the sodden, weed-choked hillock. In front of him, the land sloped downward to a pair of railroad tracks. A barbed-wire-topped chain-link fence surrounded the Miskolc District Central Postal Facility.

For the hundredth time, Németh looked at his watch. The day was already the longest of his life, and now the second hand seemed frozen in position. This glance showed that it was still five minutes to go.

Since his father had sent him to the military academy in Vienna at age twelve, he had been preparing for this day, his first military command. But all those thousands of hours of lectures and drills and maneuvers hadn't prepared him for the fear that threatened to turn his legs to jelly and loosen his bowels. He tried to run the plans for the attack through his mind again, but they faded under a huge cloud of doubt that had filled his head.

That fear and doubt had struck others; only nine of the twenty men Count László had recruited had appeared at the rendezvous. For a brief moment, a wave of relief had flooded over him because of the perfectly reasonable excuse for calling off his assigned attacks. But then he had thought of the raid on the chapel that would take place, of the fortune that was to be rescued, of the intense shame his father would feel at his failure. Németh knew he would have to carry on even if he were alone.

He checked his watch again. Two minutes to seven. He put the field glasses to his eyes. But for the scheduled Hungarian-German Solidarity Day parade, the yard outside the square three-story brick building would have been bustling with activity. Tonight, the mail-delivery trucks were parked in silent, dark rows, with only a lone guard who hadn't strayed from the radio in his shed by the gate. Beyond, lights burned only on the first floor of the building that held tens of thousands of letters and parcels that would never reach their destinations.

Pal replaced the glasses in their case and looked around him. Two men, instead of four, had been sent fifteen minutes earlier to position Gideon's ingenious nail mines alongside the road leading to the front gate. Of the seven men remaining on the hillock, four, not seven, would slide underneath the parked trucks to open the draincocks of the gasoline tanks and place pipe grenades in the pools of liquid. As planned, he and three men would penetrate the building itself.

As for the retreat to the truck that was to take them to their second attack, he could not spare a single man to substitute for the planned six. That was the least of his concerns, for he did not expect to live through the first assault.

His watch, after what seemed like an eternity, finally read seven o'clock. For an instant his stomach spasmed and he felt engulfed by an overwhelming lassitude caused by fear. Then he pushed himself up and gave the signal.

The men, born and raised in the rugged Carpathian Mountains, surefootedly and silently made their way down the slope, over the track and through the hole they'd earlier cut in the chain fence. Inside the yard, four men peeled off toward the trucks. Németh and the other three sprinted to the door by the metal-shuttered loading docks.

Németh listened for a second. He heard the faint sound of martial music, probably a radio broadcast of the parade. He put his hand on the knob, turned it slowly, then pushed.

He sprinted up the short stairs two steps at a time. Two stunned watchman had been playing cards at a desk at the far end of the loading area. One started to reach for a pistol at his belt. In one smooth, unconscious motion, Pál dropped to one knee, grabbed his right wrist with his left hand, sighted the Roth-Steyr pistol, and fired.

A black hole blossomed in the forehead of the watchman. Then he slumped to the floor.

The other watchman flung his arms into the air, his eyes wide with terror. Németh ran forward. With a length of cord he took from his belt, he began tying the man to the chair.

One of the other men called out from the loading bay, where a single gas pump stood. "Pál, it's locked."

"The key." Pál said to the watchman.

The man looked at him uncomprehendingly.

Pál yanked him to his feet, pulling him forward toward the edge of the dock until he could point at the pump. "The key," he repeated in his bad Hungarian.

This time the man understood. He nodded toward the desk. In the flat top drawer Pál found a key tied to a block of wood. He tossed it to his men, who unlocked the pump and began filling jerry cans with gasoline.

Németh made sure the watchman was secured, then went through the double doors that led to the main area of the building. The first floor was filled with row after row of wooden cubbyholes, in front of which were stacks of mail and empty stools in which sorting clerks sat during

78

the day. The men came in behind him, moving down the aisles dousing the paper and wood with gasoline.

While they worked, Pál dashed up the stairs. He placed pipe grenades at key points along the windows. On his way back down, he lit long fuses. The holes created by the explosions would act as chimneys, pulling the blaze upward.

When he got back to the first floor, the air was thick and foul with petroleum fumes.

"Let's go," he ordered. They ran through the doors out to the loading area. Németh cut the bonds of the watchman, grabbed him by the elbow, and pulled him along as they went down the stairs to the yard outside.

"Go," Pál ordered the watchman.

The man stared with wide eyes.

"I am not going to shoot you. Go."

The man took off for the sentry booth at a run. Németh, sure that the man would do as expected and sound the alarm, pulled a grenade from his belt, ran back up the stairs, lit the fuse, and tossed the grenade into the main work area.

He was sprinting across the yard when the grenade exploded. It was followed by a roar like being caught in the middle of a thunderstorm. By the time he reached the hole in the fence, the grenades on the upper floors had detonated, and glass and brick fragments rained down like hail on the yard.

Pál waited until he was back up on top of the hillock before he flopped to the ground and turned back to look. Through the holes that had once been windows he could see the fire dancing like a maddened dragon. The blaze lit the surrounding yard like day, so he could see clearly where the watchman and guard had opened the front gates and run out in the road to await help.

In the distance Pál heard the wail of sirens. A police vehicle roared into the yard, skidding to a stop just inside the gates. Moments later, two fire trucks followed, then more police.

Németh stood and gave the sign to a man stationed by the fence. The man lit a grenade and tossed it under the nearest truck.

The explosion touched off others that quickly built into a roaring firestorm. Trucks bounced, then shattered like toys. Even a hundred yards away the heat was so intense Pál had to avert his face. When the first wave passed, he saw that the police cars and fire trucks had ignited. A lone figure completely engulfed in flames staggered like a drunk toward the gate, then collapsed, writhing, on the ground.

The wait for the army was five minutes and seemed an hour. Németh saw the headlights of the first of a convoy of canvas-covered personnel carriers that must have been pulled away from the parade. He pulled out his pistol and fired twice into the air.

The first military vehicle stopped right in front of the gates, which were now blocked by the burning fire equipment. Soldiers were jumping from the back when the first of Gideon's infernal antipersonnel mines detonated from the side of the road.

Instantly, the canvas covering of the truck shredded in a deluge of shrapnel, and the night was filled with unholy shrieks from wounded men. Then a second mine detonated, and a third.

The surviving soldiers crawled off the road behind the trucks and started pouring a hail of fire into the bushes. By that time, Németh's two men were running up the hillock to his side.

When Németh saw them, he jumped up and said, "Let's get out of here."

They raced down the other side of the hillock and across a broad field to the road where their truck was parked. Pál was so exhilarated he felt as if he were flying.

The operation couldn't have gone better. Suddenly all those formal, stylized military operations he'd studied seemed strangely irrelevant. He had a clear image of what the coming war would be like. Armed and supplied by money from the sale of the treasure Gideon was recapturing, the resistance could strike blow after blow like this until the last influences of the Fascists were banished from the land. Pál Németh had never wanted to live more, to be a leader of that glorious movement.

He was so lost in thought that he almost ran over the

man who suddenly stepped out from the shadow of the truck. He nearly fired before a voice said, "Pál, it's In'Hout."

Németh was stunned. "Why are you here?"

"Gideon sent me. He needs you and your men. There's trouble."

Németh gritted his teeth. "Let's go."

9

THE PHOENIX TEAM reached the gates without incident. Charvey emerged from the sentry booth to let them inside.

"Any activity?" Gideon asked.

"The lone gendarme outside the door. That is all."

Gideon said to Ian, "We've got to cut off the telephone. There're two wires on that pole over there. By the look of the phone wire I ripped out in the booth, the one to cut is brown and braided. Can you get up there and do it?"

"Watch me," Ian said. He hurried to the pole and began shinnying up.

Gideon watched him anxiously as he reached the top, took out his knife, and sliced a wire. Then he exhaled in relief. The chapel windows and floodlights were still lit, so the guards inside wouldn't be warned. And the phone shouldn't work. Shouldn't. But there was no guarantee until somebody tried using one.

"How are we going to get the guard?" Brusilov asked.

Gideon said, "Charvey, get into the greatcoat and boots of one of the sentries. Start walking toward the loading dock very slowly, keeping your head down so the guard doesn't get a good look. Brusilov and I will flank you in the shadows."

"Got it."

While he went to change, Gideon said to Kinelly, "Oscar, I want you and Ian to circle around to the front after we've secured the docks. I hope those lights on upstairs mean a few curators are working late. If so, don't bother them. But be ready in case of trouble."

They nodded as Charvey came back from the bushes. He started down the road, covering nearly half the distance before the gendarme noticed him. The guard stood erect, puzzled. He called out, "What is it?"

Charvey continued walking, his right hand tightening around the handle of the Luger in the pocket of the greatcoat.

The guard at the door stared suspiciously for a moment longer. Then he flicked his cigarette away and reached for the strap of his Mannlicher rifle slung on his back.

"*Álljon meg!*" Gideon commanded, stepping out into the light.

The guard whirled and froze as he saw the menacing twin barrels of Gideon's shotgun.

Before he could recover, Charvey had sprung forward to strip him of his rifle. Gideon prodded the guard in the stomach toward the door.

The soldier hesitated at the door. Gideon, grimacing, poked him in the gut again, and the soldier, licking dry lips, fumbled behind him for the handle. The instant the latch clicked open, Charvey spun the soldier around and pushed him roughly ahead of them, the door flinging wide as the soldier reeled stumbling inside. Charvey and Gideon rushed in at his heels, twisting to the left, the shotguns like extensions of their bodies as they swept the warehouse in firing positions.

The interior was lit by bare bulbs dangling every few yards from the rafters. The lights glowed above long rows of paintings, prints, drawings, and statuary, many of them crated; shelves of gold, silver, and porcelain figures; an area stacked with fine antique furniture. At the back were two sets of steps, a short step leading down to double doors, another winding staircase leading upward to the high floors. At the front, by the dock door, was a pigeon-hole desk.

Two more gendarmes had been lounging at the desk, one sitting in the desk chair reading a magazine, the other on an antique stool cleaning his rifle. Both of them froze, their faces slack with astonishment, as the first soldier staggered past them. Then slowly, in complete silence, they stood, their hands raised.

Gideon's eyes never wavered from the trio, though he heard the scuffling of boots behind him. He knew it was Brusilov and Eliska coming in, while Kinelly and Ian ran around to the front.

"Get their weapons," he told Charvey.

The Frenchman moved to the two at the desk, staying clear of Gideon's line of fire in case of trouble. Brusilov and Eliska moved around Gideon and deeper inside, flanking Charvey with their own weapons leveled as well. Gideon kept particularly close watch on the soldier they'd shoved through the door. He might have been slow on the uptake, but he wasn't showing fear now. He looked like a man who'd dearly love to repay them at the first opportunity.

Gideon was determined not to give him the chance. "We're going to put these three to work. We've got to get this place cleaned out fast. Marcel, open one of those loading bay doors and unfasten the tailgate of the trunk outside. Eliska?"

She came up next to him.

"I want you to point out the most valuable objects. We'll load them first. And warn these three in Hungarian that a false twitch of a muscle will get them blasted."

Once again Gideon was impressed with Eliska's presence in a tight situation. She barked a brisk command to the three gendarmes in a voice that made her appear every inch the battle-hardened commando. Then, like a drill sergeant, she set the men to work.

With the none too gentle prodding of Gideon and the assistance of the muscular Charvey, the first truck was rapidly filled with paintings, gold, silver, and porcelain. They had started on the second truck when Eliska said to Gideon, "The furniture is bulky, so we should save that for last, if we have room. We've loaded most of the smaller things in this area. There must be other galleries with the icons, coin collections, tapestries, and carvings."

"Let's ask our friends here," Gideon said.

As they started forward, Brusilov fired his shotgun.

Gideon coiled, pivoting on the ball of his foot so he could see what was happening.

All hell had broken loose. Six soldiers had innocently stepped through the upper door in the back, and were coming down the stairs to the warehouse. They weren't Hungarians, Gideon realized in a split second's glance. They were wearing black field jackets and black breeches tucked into calf-high black jackboots. One had on an officer's peaked cap with its silver skull emblem winking in the dull light. The dress Gideon recognized as that of the *Ausgehanzug*—the "walking out" dress uniform—of the dreaded SS Totenkopfverbända, Hitler's Schutzstaffel Death's Head Troops, who guarded the concentration camps and carried out political operations in occupied countries like Poland and Czechoslovakia.

In his instant of stunned recognition, Gideon fired reflexively, joining Brusilov and the others as they poured fire at the Germans. All Gideon could figure was that Hitler must have invaded Hungary; what the fuck else would these Nazis be doing in the chapel?

The six SS troopers paused only for a second before reacting, their faces registering surprise as they swiftly unholstered their Lugers and began blasting in response. The first gendarme clawed for his own pistol, while the two that had been stationed at the desk lunged across the room toward their rifles.

Charvey reloaded, then swiveled to mow down both gendarmes as they reached the desk, while Eliska coolly shot their remaining comrade through the head. Then they bounded after Brusilov and Gideon, who were racing toward the back steps, loosening such a fusillade as they ran that the Nazis scrambled up the flight of stairs and slammed the door at the top shut. Two dead and a third badly wounded were left sprawling on the stairs, and Gideon heard the cry of a fourth when he shattered the door's panels with a single blast.

Brusilov crashed through the door, stumbling over the fallen Nazi. He cursed, then spotted the machine pistol lying next to the fallen man. He cried with glee, dropped his shotgun, and seized the MP40.

Gideon had vaulted past him, spraying the dim hallway

beyond, blasting away at muzzle flashes as stone fragments from the old walls lanced about him. Faintly he heard Kinelly's voice bellowing from deeper in the chapel proper, and he veered toward the sound, motioning for the three behind him to spread out.

He entered a wide pillared gallery, in which more gendarmes and SS troops were swarming in alarm, firing at the two fleeting figures heading in from the front entrance. Gideon caught a quick glance of Kinelly and Ian before they ducked behind the large statue of a saint. Again he heard the Irishman's bull-roaring curses, but then the voice was lost in a fresh eruption of fire, lead, and pellets whistling and ricocheting in showers of flinty sparks.

Gideon started triggering selectively, not wanting to waste shells, but not afraid to spend them either, his shotgun blasting regularly. Smoke stung his nostrils and smarted his eyes. He knew that the vital elements of silence and surprise were blown to hell now, and the only thing saving the team was his spur-of-the-moment decision to send Kinelly and Ian through the front entrance. The resultant pincers movement was momentarily bottling the defenders inside the chapel, preventing them from getting out to their trucks or cars to summon help. The team's one chance lay in pressing fast and mercilessly, for it was merely a matter of time before some of the defenders escaped or picked off team members with lucky shots.

It certainly had been bad luck, Gideon thought bitterly, that they had to mount a raid the one evening the chapel was hosting a squad of Death's Head killers. Snarling with pent-up rage and frustration, he yelled, "Close in, Kinelly."

"Close in, my bleedin' arse!" Kinelly shouted back, sprinting closer in a zigzag, firing from the hip. He made it across the open space and ducked behind the pillar where Gideon had taken cover.

"This joint is crawling with krauts," Kinelly growled. "You should see the fleet of Mercedes parked out in front. We've been sold out."

"If this had been planned, there would be more of

them," Gideon said. "And the SS wouldn't be wearing their party duds."

"We'll give them a party to remember," Kinelly growled, grinning viciously. Then he burst from cover to make a swift pass for the main stairway to the upper stories. There was a gleam of metal as a gun barrel poked from the mezzanine railing. Kinelly took a shot clean through the biceps, but managed to get off a blast toward the shooter above. The railing splintered and the German toppled over, crashing down on a gendarme whose rifle had been aimed at Gideon.

The wounded Irishman lunged up the stairs, propelled by seething hatred of the fancy black uniforms. By a fluke, his insane charge coincided with a lull in the fire fight; weapons were empty, and for a breathing space clips and cartridges were being crammed in fast. Gideon sprang after him, dispatching the gendarme with a quick shot. Ian followed.

A wave of strafing fire engulfed Kinelly when he reached the landing, but as if blessed, he tore into the corridor unscathed. Two noncom Germans in his path slumped across hastily overturned tables they'd been using for cover. A third, an officer, drooped awkwardly against a doorjamb, his pistol arching back into the room behind him as a shotgun blast tore him apart.

Plunging past the shattered bodies, Gideon could hear the battle resounding up the stairs from below. He winced inwardly at the sound of the soldiers letting loose volley after volley, yet felt gratified by the echoing reports of the team. Charvey, Eliska, and especially Brusilov with his MP40 were more than holding their own as they raked the defenders with withering fire. Those in the fore dropped so abruptly that those in the rear were blocked from escaping or countering. They were retreating under the ruthless onslaught, floundering in fear and confusion.

On the floor above, Kinelly, Gideon, and Ian continued forcing their way across the length of the chapel, moving lethally through a series of small private galleries, storerooms, and offices. They were met by a dwindling number of soldiers, who were desperately trying to train their weapons and rally a defense. Panic-stricken men, balding and paunchy in vested suits, scurried like mice for shelter, often as not getting in the way of their defenders. A few terrified and shrieking women added to the chaotic din.

Kinelly acting as point and Ian protecting their backs, the three stormed from room to room. Bullets whined about them, riddling pictures and gouging furniture and spraying chips from statues like shrapnel. An ambushing salvo finally caught Kinelly in the thigh. He couldn't be stopped, however, remaining upright to snap new shells into his shotgun.

The lurking SS officer who'd shot him leaped out cursing in an angling dash. Before Kinelly could finish reloading, the officer had fired again. But in his maddened rush, he missed at virtually point-blank range. Ian was momentarily pinned down, firing at a dimly visible SS trooper. Gideon, his shotgun empty and his Luger tucked in his belt, dove into the officer, knocking him aside and ruining his next shot. Then, jabbing the officer in the throat with the muzzle of his shotgun, Gideon grabbed the officer's pistol by its barrel, wrenched it free, and swung. Its heavy butt mashed the black peaked cap with such force that the scalp beneath it spurted crimson.

Using the officer's pistol Gideon kept the remaining defenders at bay long enough to slide two shells into his shotgun. A gendarme and an overstuffed curator went down kicking in the next few seconds under the roaring twin explosions of his weapon. Ian's target suddenly grew a gigantic hole where his belly had been. Kinelly was still walking, leaving a trail of red droplets of blood as he pumped rounds at anything that moved.

Slumping at last, breathing heavily through his mouth, Kinelly nodded. Gideon and Ian surged on along the last section of the corridor, automatically firing into each connecting room, until they reached its end. They plunged into the chapel's main administration office.

It was an imposing room, carpeted and draped, with bookcases and paintings and windows overlooking the Sajó River. The acrid stench of gunsmoke swirled in the room with the orange flashes of firing. A plump, bearded executive, rearing pompously from behind a Louis XVI desk, collapsed into his padded chair from a single shot-gun blast, his clawing fingers slipping from a pistol in his lap. Another man, taller and wearing a pince-nez, hurled a Florentine dagger, then staggered backward against a marble bust of Maria Theresa, screaming hideously as blood gushed from a neck wound. An SS man, raked by Ian, slammed into a bookcase, shattering its glass doors, dead before he hit the carpet. A wounded officer, an *Oberführer*—a brigadier—wrapped his arms around Gideon's legs. Ian brought his pistol down in a short arc; the German slumped comatose.

Then, abruptly, the carnage was over. Two gendarmes dropped their weapons. A mustached man in a pinstripe suit cowered in a corner whimpering, and a youthful clerk had his garter-sleeved arms lifted as high as he could stretch them. A blond Rubenesque woman crouched sobbing by the desk.

Swiftly, Gideon collected the weapons and locked them in a storage closet. Pocketing the key, he backed to the door and stood, listening intently. The bedlam that had reigned in the chapel's ground floor had also ended. In its hushed aftermath, all he could hear was the vague groaning of the wounded, interspersed with loud French and Russian swearing, as Charvey and Brusilov rounded up the survivors.

"Herd these people downstairs," Gideon told Ian. "And collect any of the others who're fit to walk as you go along." Then, turning, he hurried back to the gallery where they'd left Kinelly.

Kinelly was back on his feet. When Gideon approached, he was in the midst of a conversation with Charvey, while Charvey applied a tourniquet to his right leg. He was calling down an impressive array of Irish curses on the SS.

Gideon pressed by, reached the bottom of the stairs, then stopped to think, his mind racing. Time was against them. They were behind schedule, and even if the phones were in fact out, the noisy furor of the combat could well have attracted notice from the guards at the access road a kilometer away. Not to mention the chance of another SS delegation happening to visit. That meant maximum speed. They had to put the survivors to work loading the rest of the collection.

Gideon ordered Brusilov, Charvey, and Ian to gather the survivors downstairs in the large warehouse, then dispose of any remaining weapons in a lockable storage vault. He started to look for something as a crutch for Kinelly when the Irishman groused. "I'm no bloody cripple. The bastards didn't even hit the bone. My bloody arm's stiffened up, though, so you'll have to do all the lifting."

Gideon shook his head, smiling. "Get out to the trucks, you crazy mick."

"I'm beginning to wish they'd got him in the mouth," Ian said.

Kinelly took a swipe at him, them limped off. Ian went to join Brusilov and Charvey.

Gideon spotted Eliska slumped into a chair by the gallery door, her head in her hands. He rushed over to her, squatted, then asked with concern, "Were you hit?"

Eliska shook her head. Gideon could hear her quietly sobbing.

"What's the matter?" he asked gently.

She didn't reply for a moment. Then she took a deep breath. When she looked up, her face was white and she was trembling. "It's . . . it's just . . ." Her voice trailed off as she swept her arm out toward the room.

For the first time, Gideon was aware how much like a charnel house the gallery looked. It was a gore-splattered shambles, blood staining the walls and rivuleting across the floor to coagulate in puddles. The air was noxious, a murk of acrid smoke and gritty dust. Bodies lay sprawled with gaping mouths and sightless eyes, or feebly convulsed in slumped positions.

Eliska spoke again. "While . . . while it was happening, I couldn't think. I just reacted. Then, when it was over, I realized what I'd done."

Gideon took her hand. "I know," he said. "I felt the same way after my first battle. What you should concentrate on is the fact that this mission would have been a failure a long time ago without you."

Eliska looked at him a moment. Then she stood. "I'm all right now. Let's get on with it."

Gideon started to turn away. Eliska stopped him, saying, "Scott. Thank you."

He nodded. Then he said, "We've got to get a move on."

Downstairs in the main warehouse, the survivors, though stunned and bewildered, were ferrying material from two smaller galleries to the trucks.

"The second truck is nearly full," Brusilov reported. "We've got all the gold and silver. Now we're going to—"

At that instant, two machine guns opened up, strafing the loading dock with a torrent of death. A crimson line stitched across the forehead of a woman in a long green evening gown, and she jerked like a puppet on a string before collapsing. A fat man in a too tight uniform was blown off his feet when the porcelain bust he was carrying shattered into a million pieces. The air was full of flying art objects as the other terrified survivors scattered for cover.

Brusilov hit the floor next to Gideon. He screamed, "We've got to get the floodlights!"

Gideon nodded. They rose to a squat, then lunged forward. Machine-gun bullets tore up the concrete around them as they dove out the loading bay door. They landed on their backs, firing upward at the bulbs.

Then the loading docks went dark. Gideon crawled to the edge, getting cover behind the raised tailgate of the nearest Mercedes truck. Brusilov joined him.

"Hold your fire!" Gideon yelled to the rest of the team. "Hold your fire!"

"Why?" Brusilov asked.

"No use wasting ammunition. And the less we provoke fire, the more undamaged objects we'll have."

"You think they're from the roadblock?" Brusilov asked.

Gideon nodded. "No other troops could have made it that fast. I was afraid of this."

He cautiously turned and looked around the corner of the truck. By the barrel flashes from the occasional machine-gun bursts he could tell the Hungarians were set up by the gate, where they could sweep the entire lot and building.

Gideon ran the limited options through his mind. A frontal assault across the flat hundred-yard expanse with no cover was suicidal. They could go back up through the chapel and out the front, but that would mean abandoning the mission. And every minute they stayed put, reinforcements were most likely moving closer, cutting down on their already small chance of escape.

Brusilov seemed to read his mind. "Not unlike the canyon, my friend," he said. "We are once again cornered."

"I'm open to suggestions," Gideon said.

"The Bolsheviks, what they would do is herd those people inside. That way they could hide behind them, and in the confusion—"

"We're not going to do that," Gideon said, adding, "But as they say, you only live once, so—"

"I am with you," Brusilov interjected.

They leaped to their feet, quickly checking their weapons.

"On three," Gideon said. "One . . . two . . . three."

They jumped out from behind the trucks and down to the ground four feet below the dock. Brusilov had just unleashed a loud Russian yell when he stopped in his tracks.

They saw the blinding light of the explosion a second before the deafening roar and the shock of the blast swept over them. Then came a second explosion, and Gideon saw a machine gun and two men go flying into the air.

The crackle of rifle fire followed, then a military car exploded like a firecracker. There were a few more random shots, then, except for the sound of flames, silence.

"About time that bloody Dutchman got here."

Gideon turned around to see Kinelly on the edge of the loading dock. "Get those people inside back to work," he ordered. Then he ran toward the gate.

Gideon got there as Brusilov engulfed the slender In'Hout with a huge bear hug. Next to him was Pál Németh, a huge, proud smile on his face.

Gideon shook his hand. "Great job," he said.

"We had to outrun a police car," Németh said. "I'm

afraid we attracted some attention. And we could hear fighting a couple kilometers away."

"That means we'd better get our asses in gear," Gideon said. He ran back to the dock and ordered Charvey and Ian to lock up the remaining prisoners. He turned to Eliska. "Whatever we have in the two trucks is going to have to be it."

Eliska nodded. "We have the most valuable goods. It is far more than I'd hoped."

Gideon smiled grimly. "Now let's hope these trucks start."

10

THE MERCEDES TRUCKS started, and as a bonus they were fully fueled. The only problem, Gideon realized as he maneuvered the first one past the wreckage of the Hungarian military cars and down the access road, was they were far less powerful than the huge Czech Tatra they had planned to use.

At the main highway, Gideon turned right. He pulled to a halt down the road where the Tatra and the two other moving vans had been left.

Gideon jumped out of the cab and went back to talk to Pál Németh. "Why don't you pull these trucks onto the road? That'll slow down the pursuit. You can make your way back to town from here."

"I've got a better idea," Németh said. "My men and I will lead them on a chase. They will expect us to head north toward the mountains, and when they see signs of trucks heading that way they will follow. If they catch up to us, we'll blow up the trucks in the road and fade into the countryside."

Gideon was silent, marveling at the transformation he saw in the young Slovak aristocrat. Németh was no longer the green cadet; he spoke with the confidence of the proven leader of men.

Gideon said, "Good idea. You and your men have performed like professional soldiers. You have our thanks."

"We do not want thanks. All we want is the weapons and military supplies the sale of the wealth in those trucks

94

can buy. While we wait, we will be recruiting and training other freedom fighters. We will make the Fascists pay in blood for their greed."

Gideon shook the young man's hand a final time. Then he climbed back in the cab and put the Mercedes in gear.

The ten kilometers to the cutoff to Debrecen was a smooth, flat highway. As Gideon made the turn south, he saw in the rear-view mirror the three trucks driven by Németh's men pull to a halt. They would wait until the Hungarians were near before leading them off. That vital assistance would delay the pursuit long enough, Gideon hoped.

His confidence was dimmed somewhat by the sad state of the new road. Although it was a major route, the surface was full of chuckholes and bumps. As they approached a small section of mountainous terrain, the two-lane highway narrowed, becoming winding and treacherous.

Gideon drove with one hand clamped on the steering wheel and the other on the gearshift knob, the truck whining and complaining as it pulled its overweight load across the high, rough land. This was old land, he thought; an ancient wilderness of rock and ledge and crevice, the skyline a distortion of dips and rises veiled by night and weather and antiquity. A cruel and unforgiving land; he couldn't wait to get out of it.

A half hour later, they crossed the summit of bleak, jagged heights and started the gradual descent that would eventually lead to the Alföld, the great Hungarian plain. Gideon felt a slight sense of relief now, the worst of the driving evidently behind them. But he didn't relax; they weren't out of the hills yet, and the road was still a rutted hazard.

They entered a round-shouldered valley that shortly squeezed into a canyon, and soon the canyon funneled into a narrow, precipitously sloped gorge. Centuries dry, the gorge showed erosive marks where once a river had churned its course. Now it was only a thin, deep pass, harboring torrent-strewn boulders and cataract-gouged ridges, some hardy scrub and a few gnarled conifers, and the cracked, twisted ribbon of the highway.

Slowing to protect the truck's groaning suspension, Gideon followed the old river's serpentine passage. Roughly midway through it, he rounded a bend and saw two Skoda sedans dead ahead, parked grille-to-grille in a blockading wedge across both lanes.

He instantly saw that he couldn't swing around them. The sheer wall on his right flanked too close, almost abutting the pavement's edge, and on his left, where there was enough room, was the rest of the roadblock. Sandbags were piled lining the shoulder, along with a four-ton canvas-topped army truck. Gideon couldn't identify the truck's make because the roadblock was shrouded in gloom, the only illumination gleaming from flashlights and the dim, slit-shielded headlamps of the sedans. Otherwise it was all dark, no doubt on purpose to avoid forewarning its presence. But there was no mistaking the Toldi light tank that was parked parallel to the cars, backed in a wide spot between the misshapen boulders, and facing the road with a machine gun and what appeared to be a short-barreled 20mm cannon.

Eliska was in the seat next to Gideon. She asked in a hoarse voice, "How did they get here so fast?"

"Maybe these guys were going somewhere, got the message, and decided to set up a block in case we came along," Gideon downshifted a gear and floored the accelerator. "Maybe they're not here for us at all."

Hungarian infantrymen were racing to their positions, most diving behind the sandbags, while others crouched by the sedans, aiming the rifles, the few with flashlights flagging their arms. The tank crew, distinctive in their overalls, double-breasted coats, and leather helmets, bolted for the open-hatched Toldi.

"Maybe I can bluff us through again," Eliska offered.

"I don't think so," Gideon said loudly above the revving engine. "This isn't some half-assed checkpoint like the one before."

"But we can't ram through," Eliska said. "That tank can't miss at this close range."

"Yes, but there's a chance the range is *too* close," Gideon yelled. "If the tank's carrying only explosive shells, a point-blank cannon shot would blow up their own men along with us."

Gideon's truck continued picking up speed, and the one driven by Charvey was on his tail. Nearing, Gideon could see the snouts of tripod-mounted machine guns poking from the sandbags, tracking their approach, and he wished he could warn the men in back. But he couldn't, and there wasn't enough clearance on Eliska's side of the truck for her to climb out on the running board and bang on the wooden sides.

"Get down," he shouted at Eliska, and steered to the right, angling toward the gorge wall until the front fender was grazing against the slab-sided rock. "Get down on the floor!"

He glanced over and saw Eliska hadn't moved. He grabbed her neck and forced her to the floorboards as the Hungarians opened fire.

Lead rained into the trucks first from the rifles of the crouching soldiers, then from the chattering machine guns behind the sandbags. Bullets careened off the grille, smashing the left headlight and stitching punctures along the hood and cab. Gideon's windshield shattered.

Gideon, hunched down, shifted again while he deliberately wheeled the truck scraping along the gorge wall. The right fender caved in, the side-view mirror snapped off, and the panels of the van body buckled and creased, popping their rivets. The brutal rending of metal against stone was a tortured squeal that almost drowned out the sound of the gunfire.

The sedan parked diagonally in the right lane was looming directly ahead, and Gideon knew the truck was now presenting a broadside target. He glimpsed streamers of red lancing from the tank's machine gun, and heard the tracers hammering across the left side of the truck. Shots flew thicker through the cab, one nipping his check while others plowed into the seat and fractured the glass in the passenger door. He tried to ignore it all, concentrating on keeping the entire right side of the truck in contact with the gorge.

The truck struck the sedan in its rear quarter, in line with its truck hinges. The sedan crumpled and slid sideways, its hood denting the front of the other sedan and puncturing its radiator. The truck shuddered to its core, the impact clipping off the already broken left headlamp and shearing back half of the left fender while the front end set to wobbling as if ready to shake apart. But Gideon, foot glued to the gas pedal, forced the truck to crash on through, wedging a path between the gorge and the sedan.

The enfilading gunfire rose in a crescendo, through Gideon perceived some answering shots beginning to come from Ian in the back. They were far enough along in the roadblock now to spot targets, and he could hear Brusilov's MP40 streaming lead at the army truck and the first row of sandbags.

In the splintered remains of his side-view mirror, Gideon glimpsed a sparkling silver stick arcing through the air. Pipe grenade, he realized; probably quick thinking by Brusilov, who loved grenades. The stick landed by the army truck, then another dropped behind one of the sandbag nests. Infantrymen scattered, knowing what would happen in the next second.

Two explosions, geysering flame and thunder, echoed resoundingly through the narrow gorge. The tripod of a machine gun flipped high, and the army truck ruptured into shredded canvas and flying steel shards. Soldiers were hurled, collapsing like empty sacks, though others still determinedly manned their weapons and the tank's gunner never let up his unrelenting barrage.

Shoving the battered sedan over on its side, the truck dragged it along by a snagged bumper, strewing a trail of scrap metal. Once they were past the center of the roadblock, there was increasingly less for the Hungarians to hit, mostly the trucks' rear quarter sections, tires, and doors. The tires were tucked under the frame, partially shielded by the body. When leaving the chapel, they'd chained the tailgate up like a drawbridge; if the men stayed low, they'd be fairly well protected.

Yet they weren't free and clear yet, Gideon thought, not by a long shot. For assuming his hope had been correct, and the tank carried only the common HE-type cannon shell, then he could also assume its crew would begin firing as soon as the trucks drew safely ahead. Already the turret was cranking around, and the gorge beyond stretched straight and deep. No matter how fast they drove down its narrow length, they'd be patsies for the tank, hit before they could reach the distant bend.

In'Hout had taken over Brusilov's MP40, firing continuously from the rear of the second truck. Brusilov was tossing grenades steadily, quantity making up for his inability to aim his pitches. Eruptions rocked the roadblock in a haphazard pattern, catching infantrymen and flinging them wide, while others scurried for cover, not knowing where next a stick might fall. One wild throw dropped a grenade rolling under the tank, where it burst an instant later. The tank quivered and some tread links were bent, but no real damage was done, not the disabling kind needed to kill its cannon.

Ahead, the murky stretch grew more visible as the wreckage of the army truck and the other sedan blazed like a torch to light the road unpleasantly bright. The well-trained soldiers ignored the fires, skirting past to double forward and maintain their shooting. A rain of small rocks and pebbles pattered down among them, bouncing off the pavement, evidently loosed by Brusilov's earth-quaking blasts.

The second sedan's fuel tank suddenly exploded, followed by a crackling noise. Then came another noise, a deeper, growling rumble. Gideon's initial reaction was that the cannon had fired, but instead, another hail of stones began pelting the roadblock. He leaned his head out his broken side window and saw a large boulder tumbling down the left slope above the tank. The slope was steep, but not as sheer as the wall to his right, and the boulder leaped into the air, struck again, and dislodged a greater mass of earth and rock.

"Holy shit," Gideon muttered, keeping his speed and the truck tearing along the gorge wall. Heavy fragments of stone and shale began showering down with the boulder, a rock the size of his head smashing into the middle of the truck's hood. It ricocheted off, leaving a huge dent, and smacked into the entangled sedan, jarring it free of the truck. The sedan ripped loose with a grinding howl of shorn metal. Charvey's truck smashed into it, sending the wreck tumbling to the left.

The rumbling increased until, with a loud snapping sound, the entire left slope of the gorge collapsed onto the roadblock.

Gideon saw infantrymen running for their lives. Then a vast billowing cloud fanned out over the truck, swirling in through glassless windows and flooding the cab with grit and debris, choking them and scratching their eyes. Blinded, Gideon could only drive by feel, continuing to steer against the gorge wall. The engine coughed, almost stalled, but he nursed it along.

Gradually they moved out of the cloud, and when the air had cleared to a dusty fog, Gideon realized they were well along the straightaway. Craning out to look back, he was overjoyed to see through the haze of the hovering cloud that the second truck had also escaped. The landslide, however, had completely engulfed the bed of the gorge, snuffing the fires and burying the tank. A few dazed soldiers and an exposed portion of the sedan were the only signs that a roadblock had ever existed.

"You can get up now," he called to Eliska. But he didn't stop. He veered away from the gorge wall and kept the accelerator planted flat.

The road swung along the scalloped ledge of a deep ravine. Gideon sped through the turns, caroming from lane to lane, while Eliska cringed, staring at the dropoff and the rugged ravine far below. She braced herself with both hands to keep from being tossed around.

From the ravine, the road wound through another gorge and then started a steep decline to the Alföld in a series of switchback curves. Gideon rushed on full throttle, arms and legs flailing as he double-clutched while shifting gears, pumped the brakes, and twisted a steering wheel that had developed a full half-turn of play.

"You can slow down," Eliska finally said. "We made it. There's no sense killing us now."

"Okay," Gideon said breathlessly. He slowed and said sheepishly, "I guess back there just got to me."

"It got to all of us," she replied, smiling. She leaned over and kissed him on the cheek. Gideon, touched by the impulsive display of affection, reached over and squeezed her arm. Then, with a wave back to Charvey, he accelerated to a comfortable pace.

With surprising abruptness, they dropped away from the mountainous country and emerged out into the Alföld. Gideon drove along the road that seemed an endless flat line unreeling across the windswept, barren plain. Shortly they crossed the Tisza River and passed through the tiny junction town of Polgár. Sixty kilometers left, Gideon thought. If they could maintain their pace, they'd be in Debrecen right on schedule.

Gideon looked over toward Eliska. She was gazing out the window, an amused smile on her face.

"What's so funny?" he asked.

Eliska turned to him. "I was imagining the look on Herr Doktor Posse's face about now. He's probably close to apoplexy."

"Who's he?"

"Hans Posse is the director of the Sonderauftrag Linz— the Linz Special Mission. He's in charge of stocking Hitler's Führermuseum that's being built in Linz. It's supposed to become greater than the Louvre, the National Gallery, or the Prado. Maybe it will—Austria was looted bare, especially the Rothschild mansions, and now Poland and Czechoslovakia are being looted. Dr. Posse recently arrived in Miskolc to take the cream of the collections of Count László and the other aristocrats."

"He was at the chapel?"

"Not while we were there," Eliska answered. "He would probably have been with Dr. Dworshak, whose specialty is coins and medals, and certainly with Dr. Wolffhardt, who's in the SS, and would be in command of those troopers. They're all well known in art circles, and I'd have recognized them. No, they must have already picked what they liked of the collection, then left the actual transporting to their assistants and underlings. Those are the ones we encountered, along with the curators and Hungarian soldiers."

Gideon chuckled. "We snatched the collection out from under their noses, while they were enjoying the brownshirts' parade."

"I doubt if someone like Dr. Posse would bother with that. He was probably staying outside Miskolc, vacationing at the Tapolca warm springs and baths." Eliska sighed. "I wouldn't mind a warm bath right now. I feel the way you and your men looked when I got you out of that jail."

They lapsed into silence for the remainder of the trip. Chill wind whistled through the cab, while a dusty moon bathed the surrounding plain in soft light. The low covering mass of clouds grew wispier and then vanished overhead as the cold front swept westerly.

Drawing near to Debrecen, they crossed wide vistas of irrigated fields for crops and cattle. Then, almost as abruptly as they'd emerged onto the plain, the farms and pastures fell away and they entered streets of closely packed houses and buildings.

They drove through the outskirts of Debrecen, Eliska pointing out where the fifteenth-century walls of the original town had stood when Debrecen had been a refuge against the invading Turks. Avoiding the center of the city, Eliska directed Gideon southeast, through an industrial district of machinery and furniture factories, and onto a broad street which flanked the railway yards and freight terminals.

Gideon, anticipating Eliska, headed right for what was obviously the main freight depot. It was an imposing structure, its surrounding warehouses and sidings occupying three entire blocks. He slowed, scrutinizing the area for a sign of a waiting train.

"Keep going," Eliska said. "The train will be on a more remote siding."

Gideon continued south, paralleling row after row of tracks on his left. They passed clusters of warehouses, factories, and docks; scatters of line shacks, signal towers, boxcars, and water tanks; and parked strings of dark coaches, gondolas, and flatcars. Shortly the sprawl of the railyards began tapering as the tracks linked, funneling into main lines. Gideon wondered if they'd soon be out of Debrecen altogether and wind up back out on the plain again.

Then, after the eye-watering smell of a soap works and

a tannery, they reached an open field with a white knoll some twenty feet high, the knoll evidently having been formed by years of dumping rubbish and ashes. Eliska directed Gideon to bear left, skirting the knoll, toward two sooty brick warehouses that were connected by a long wooden loading platform.

Approaching, Gideon saw that the building and platform fronted a section of track siding. On the siding chugged a stubby 2-4-2 steam locomotive, with blackened blinder panels and a skinny smokestack. A spiral of steam rose lazily from its second boiler hump. Coupled to its tender was a metal-clad baggage car, and attached behind that were two coaches, the first brightly ornate in crimson and yellow, black striping, and carriage lamps, the other an ordinary passenger type with a rear observation deck. All the window blinds were drawn in both coaches, but some of the compartments, particularly in the fancy coach, were glowing with light.

"Pull up by the platform," Eliska said. "We'll unload there."

Gideon braked and exited from the cab. He saw Count László approach. At his side was Vilém, who had gone directly on to Debrecen after escorting Charvey, Ian, and Kinelly to Miskolc. When Gideon moved forward to greet the count, he saw behind him in the shadows four armed men standing guard at the steps to the coach.

The count had a broad smile on his face, for the first time Gideon could remember. "Congratulations!" he said. "I take it the mission has been a success."

"We got most of it," Gideon said.

"Did you have trouble?" the count asked.

"Take a look at the truck," Gideon said. "That'll give you an idea."

The count turned to look at the Mercedes Gideon had driven. It was now a candidate for the scrap heap. One headlight was missing, and the other had a shattered lens. All the windows were smashed, all the fenders mangled, and the dented hood flaps bowed out like a pair of broken wings. The right side was scraped bare of paint, the panels bashed in, with jagged slits and gouges and bullet holes. The left front wheel tilted and the entire body had a distinct list to it.

"I see," the count remarked after a moment. He turned back to Gideon. "This evidence adds to the distinction of your achievement. I will certainly pass on my highest praises to Monsieur Philaix."

"Skip the accolades," Gideon said. "Just get us out of Hungary."

The smile disappeared from the count's face at Gideon's dry remark. "I will do that," László said. "That is why we must transfer the contents of the trucks to the baggage car immediately."

The men riding in the backs of the trucks were stiff and sore from the rough ride. But with the exception of Kinelly, whose wounded arm was in a sling, they pitched in with László's guards.

When they finished, László said to Gideon, "It is now shortly after ten-thirty. The train will leave exactly at twelve. To avoid undue attention, the trucks must be moved."

"Where?"

"About two kilometers down the road on which you drove there is an old warehouse. Vilém will show you. You will pull the trucks inside so that they are out of sight. In the office on the first floor are clean clothes and food. I will send my car for you in one hour."

Gideon started for the Mercedes, and Eliska began to follow.

"My dear," László said, "you will stay. The facilities in my car are more appropriate for a woman."

Eliska looked at Gideon and smiled. "He is right. I have gotten so accustomed to traveling with you I didn't think."

"You did a great job," Gideon said.

Her smile widened with pleasure at the compliment. Then she turned away.

Vilém led the way in a car. Gideon followed, with Brusilov in the passenger seat.

"I am so hungry I could eat an entire cow," Brusilov said. "Two cows, maybe."

"You can relax now and concentrate on getting fat,"

Gideon said. "For the first time since we left Belgium, all we have to do is sit back and let someone else do the worrying."

"That sounds nice, my friend," Brusilov said.

The road was deserted. At the square, squat warehouse, Vilém got out of the car and opened the double doors to the inside. Gideon pulled in, followed by Charvey in the second truck.

Gideon shut off the engine. Then the garage doors closed and the inside was pitch black.

A ripple of concern went through Gideon. He opened the door of the cab and tentatively climbed out. He thought he heard the scuffle of feet, and he tensed.

The lights went on.

"That's them!" Vilém shouted.

A small horde of brownshirts holding weapons surrounded them on four sides.

A wave of blind fury seized Gideon. He whirled toward Vilém. "You fucking bastard!" he howled.

He lunged toward their betrayer. He got two steps before the butt of a rifle crashed down on his skull.

11

GIDEON'S AWAKENING SENSES first met a cold clammy stone floor and walls. As the haze began to slowly clear before his eyes, he realized that he was in a cell. The room was lit by a single bare bulb overhead. A chill wind whipped through a barred but glassless window, carrying with it the buzz of a crowd and the sounds of marching soldiers.

When he tried to move, he realized his wrists were tightly bound behind his back. To his right on the floor he could see Brusilov and Charvey were similarly tied. Noticing them bleeding from nasty cuts on their heads, Gideon became conscious of the moist, sticky blood on his own face.

Gideon thought, I must have been the last one to regain consciousness. Or maybe I was the only one knocked out. He had no idea what had happened or where he was.

Then he saw that Brusilov and Charvey were staring intently at something behind him.

"What is it?" he asked. "Where are we?"

Brusilov cast him a quick look. "Quiet!"

"What?"

Brusilov nodded toward the far corner of the cell.

Gideon tried to turn, but he was immediately punished by his wickedly throbbing head. He let the pain subside for a moment, then rolled over.

It took him a moment to realize everyone was staring

at In'Hout, who had raised himself into a sitting position away from the wall.

The first thing Gideon saw was the perspiration streaming down the Dutchman's bright-red face, as if he'd been laboring in a blazing tropical sun instead of languishing in a frigid cell. In'Hout's eyes were closed, and he was hyperventilating, breathing rapidly in and out like a bellows. Each time he exhaled, he tensed his arms and his shoulders rocked in an up-and-down motion.

The room was thick with tension. To Gideon's right, Ian and Kinelly seemed to be holding their breath, as if reserving the cell's air supply for In'Hout.

In'Hout's breathing grew louder and still more rapid, the flow of perspiration now so heavy that drops of moisture dripped steadily from his chin to the bare concrete floor. The flex of In'Hout's shoulders became so pronounced and his effort so intense Gideon found himself holding his own breath as well.

Then suddenly In'Hout let out a cry and thrust his shoulders out of joint with an audible crack. Gideon thought he'd badly hurt himself, until the shoulders snapped forward into line again. Then In'Hout's hands, free from the bonds, came into view.

"My God!" Gideon exclaimed.

In'Hout sagged forward, head on his chest, recovering from his ordeal. Gideon turned toward Ian, who anticipated the question.

"Joel told us it's a form of yoga. Houdini used the method for his escapes, and Joel's been practicing it for years."

"His shoulders seemed almost double-jointed."

"You're right," In'Hout puffed. His facial color was returning to normal. "Another key is tensing the muscles as much as possible when the rope is tied. That creates some slack when the muscles are relaxed. From there it's a matter of concentration."

"Why don't you concentrate on getting us out of here now?" Kinelly offered.

In'Hout nodded and got to his feet. As he walked to the cell door to take a look, Gideon asked, "Where are we?"

Ian replied, "I think it must be the brownshirts' headquarters. In the center of town. They brought us here in one of the Mercedes trucks. We got a glimpse of a big parade—must be the same celebration as in Miskolc."

In'Hout was now at Gideon's side. He helped him to his feet, saying, "The corridor is empty. It leads to a solid wooden door that's locked."

"Get us untied first," Gideon said. "Then we'll—"

Then all froze as they heard a door opening, then steps in the corridor.

"Quick," Gideon hissed to In'Hout. "Get back down and loop the cord around your hands behind you." A key grated in the cell door. In'Hout dove for the floor, put his hands behind his back, and leaned back in a sitting position.

Then the cell door swung inward. A brownshirt carrying a machine pistol walked in, followed by a small, thin bantam of a man dressed in a gray pinstripe suit. The man glanced haughtily around for a moment. His eye caught the Phoenix emblem on their sweaters, and he stepped closer to Gideon to inspect it.

Then he stepped back and said with a thin smile, "A bird. Very appropriate for men who fly up walls and off cliffs. Unfortunately, you seem to have flown into a coop this time."

The man spoke in German with only a trace of an accent. His tone and manner were arrogant.

"Who are you?" Gideon asked brusquely.

"Who am I?" the man sneered. "I am your captor. Gyul Dánya, deputy chairman of the Arrow Front, if you care to know. But who you are is a matter of much more interest. A motley, disreputable crew of foreign adventurers, from the look of you. Yet, also men who can achieve miracles. A prisoner is rescued from an impregnable fortress in Poland, a whole Hungarian army unit is humiliated, a fortune in heavily guarded art treasures is seized. Quite remarkable achievements."

"I don't understand," Gideon said. "You grab us and let the treasure get away, the stuff your buddy Hitler wants so badly."

The man moved closer to him, his intense eyes shining. "You do not know of what you speak. Friendship with

Germany is useful, but only as a means to our true goal—a strong, powerful Greater Hungary, all her ancestral lands restored, one true Facist state."

"But Count László . . ."

"Count László is a man of vision," Dánya interrupted. "Do you believe that those goatherders in the mountains will see a single forint from all that wealth? Bah! With that wealth and his cunning, László will serve us well in foreign capitals. For he shares our goals, and our determination to eliminate forever the influences of the Communists and the filthy Jews."

In'Hout couldn't hold in his rage. "Fucking bastard," he hissed, spitting on the floor.

Dánya wheeled to face him. He stood in front of In'Hout with his hands clasped behind his back, rocking on his toes and heels, looking him up and down in mock inspection.

"A Jew," he finally said, his voice dripping with contempt. "The Germans will be interested that one of you was a Jew."

Gideon knew what was coming. Out of the corner of his eye he located the armed guard, who was intently watching his leader.

"Yes," Dánya continued. "My men will take special delight in killing a Jew. We will see that—"

In'Hout sprang upward, his powerful hands reaching for Dánya's throat.

Gideon was ready. He hurled himself to the side and back, his shoulder socking with vicious force into the brownshirt's stomach, inches below the breastbone. The guard let out a loud whoosh of air, then slammed into the stone wall. Before he could recover his balance, Charvey tucked and rolled, knocking the man's feet out from under him. The guard fell, and an instant later Brusilov dove on him, smothering his face with his massive chest. The brownshirt kicked and flailed desperately, then went limp.

When Gideon turned, he saw that Dánya's eyes were bulging out of their sockets, his face had turned blue, and blood trickled out of the corner of his mouth. Then In'Hout flexed his rock-hard gymnast's forearms a final time. Gideon heard a sharp crack, and Dánya slumped lifelessly to the floor.

In'Hout was breathing hard as he stared down at the body that looked like a grotesque broken doll. Gideon came up to him and said, "You got your revenge, and you deserved it, Joel."

"A man can take only so much," In'Hout said. He continued staring for a moment. Then he looked up at Gideon. "Let's get out of here."

In'Hout bent and patted Dánya's body without finding a weapon. He moved to the guard, who had a pistol as well as the MP40 that had clattered to the floor of the cell. In'Hout removed the weapons and a key to the cell.

When In'Hout stood, he said to Gideon, "No knife. Turn around and let me see if I can work the knots free."

"No time for that," Gideon said. "What's down that corridor? Did you get a look at it when they brought you in?"

"A kind of orderly room, with a couple desks and file cabinets," In'Hout said. "On the other side of the stairs I got a quick look at what seemed to be a bunk room."

"How many guards?"

"A dozen brought us in," In'Hout replied. "I hope they've gone to watch the parade."

"We'll find out," Gideon said, adding, "You'll have to take both weapons, Joel."

"Give me the pistol," Kinelly said.

The Irishman's left arm had been tied behind his back to his belt. The brownshirts hadn't touched the arm that was in a sling.

"Can you use that arm?" Gideon asked.

"If I have to."

In'Hout gave him the Luger and led the way out of the cell. They moved down the corridor, light-footed as pumas. They halted by the solid wooden door.

Snatches of laughter, talk, and music filtered through. They couldn't tell how many men were in the room beyond.

In'Hout looked at Gideon, who shrugged as if to say, We have no choice. In'Hout quietly fitted the key into the door, then turned and shoved.

Three brownshirts inside were caught by surprise. In'Hout swung the butt of the machine pistol at one sitting on the edge of the desk by the door. The man moved enough to deflect the blow, then grabbed the weapon, pulling In'Hout to the floor.

Gideon tripped over them, unable to keep his balance with his hands tied behind his back. A stocky, unshaven brownshirt kicked him viciously in the ribs as he fumbled at the flap of his holster. He was pulling the pistol free when Charvey snapped a vicious kick to his groin. The man doubled over. Charvey unleashed another kick that caught the soft spot of the man's throat, under the ear. The brownshirt crumpled, then vomited. Instantly, Charvey stamped the heel of his boot on the back of the man's skull, and he heard the twiglike snapping of splintering facial bones.

A man sitting with his feet up on the desk, leaning back on the rear two legs of his chair, had been the slowest to react. Brusilov crouched and gave the desk a shove. The brownshirt tumbled backward, cracked his head against the edge of a metal file cabinet, then was still.

In'Hout and his husky opponent had tumbled over and over toward the far side of the room. In'Hout landed on top, and exerting all of his strength, pressed the machine pistol closer and closer to his enemy's throat. The man began to gag.

A bare-chested man with shaving cream on half of his face appeared in the doorway. He grabbed In'Hout's hair, jerked his head back, and raised a gleaming straight razor in his right hand.

At the instant the soldier's hand began to fall, a shot rang out. The man's body jerked convulsively up on his toes as the bullet from Kinelly's Luger tore a hole in his skull. Another shot cracked through the room and the brownshirt In'Hout had been wrestling with fell backward with a deep grunt.

There was silence for a moment. Then Kinelly said, "I guess the arm works."

"Good job," Gideon said. "Cut us free with that razor before help arrives."

111

In'Hout picked up the razor and cut their bonds while Brusilov scavanged another MP40. Charvey and Ian found pistols, but that was the extent of the weapons.

"I guess I'm left with the razor," Gideon said. Then he opened the door to the stairway and started to descend.

The front doors of the building were open, and from outside came the amplified voice of an impassioned speaker haranguing in Hungarian. Two brownshirts leaned against the doorway listening, and Gideon could see the backs of others sitting on the steps outside.

Gideon called Brusilov and In'Hout forward. They crept down the steps, getting halfway before a brownshirt heard a noise and turned.

Brusilov and In'Hout opened fire, spraying the backs of the brownshirts, the volleys of lead flinging the men in all directions. Then the team dashed headlong down the remaining steps and out into the street.

The few seconds of intense gunfire had alerted the large throng that jammed the street to listen to the Arrow Front rally. Heads spun with alarm, uncertain what the noise was or where it had come from.

The team rammed into the crowd, knocking the closest bystanders aside. They stumbled into others, shouting, touching off a chain reaction of panicky jostling. A knot of brownshirts elbowed after them. One, jumping for Kinelly, was sent spinning by Charvey's pistol. A second did a nosedive as Ian shot him, and a third dropped into the gutter, riddled by In'Hout's automatic weapon.

Brusilov fired into the air to create more chaos. Screams of high-pitched hysteria followed as the crowd broke and scattered, people trampling over each other in their frantic haste to find cover.

The Phoenix team broke free of the crowd, Brusilov leading the way down an empty side street. He slowed at the next intersection, waiting to hear which way to go.

Gideon pulled up beside him and chanced a look at his watch. "Ten to twelve," he said urgently. "We still have time to catch the train."

"Which way?"

Gideon looked up. The moon was ahead of them, a silvery coin on the horizon.

"The moon was descending ahead of us when we drove to the station," Gideon said. "We must be headed in approximately the right direction. But we need transportation."

"We'll have to look for a—"

Brusilov flinched as a bullet smacked into the wall beside him. Other shots followed, and they saw a pack of brownshirts sprinting toward them. They took off as In'Hout hung back to unleash a volley into the swarm. One brownshirt's head snapped backward, a second tumbled with arms outflung. Two more rolled across the pavement, clawing and kicking.

In'Hout turned and ran to catch up with the others as the remaining brownshirts kept up the chase. Sirens whined in the town as the authorities began to react.

The Phoenix team approached a threeway intersection, where a bus was pulling away. Brusilov stopped, aimed, and fired off a short burst that shattered the rearview window. The driver slammed on the brakes. Brusilov ran up, pulled the doors open, grabbed the astonished driver, and threw him down into the street. The rest of the team scrambled aboard. Brusilov rammed the bus into gear and accelerated as shots shattered the rear windows. A handful of terrified passengers crammed themselves under seats, whimpering.

Brusilov kept his foot on the floor as the bus careened down the rutty street. Then Gideon tapped him on the shoulder and said, "Over there. Make a left somewhere. We should aim for that smokestack."

"What?"

"The tannery we spotted coming into town. It's right by the siding."

They were paralleling the tracks to their right. They passed a string of warehouses, a lumber yard, then more warehouses. Then they saw up ahead a white knoll that rose like a moonlit beacon.

The road ended at a field. Gideon led the way across the flat, empty ground. He skirted the knoll of ashes and came to a stop beside a wooden paling fence. On the other side of the fence a long open stretch led up to the

113

two brick warehouses and the loading platform that fronted the siding on which rested László's special train.

"*Mon Dieu,* we're in time," Charvey gasped.

Suddenly the locomotive whistled, and somebody at the other end of the train shouted something in reply. The locomotive quickened its chugging, and Ian, busily prying loose the bottom crossboard of the fence, snarled, "We haven't caught it yet. Help me."

Charvey bent, and together they wrenched the board off. The team crawled through single-file.

Gideon stood, staring at the locomotive, which continued to build up a head of steam.

"You got any ideas?" Brusilov asked.

"How are we fixed for ammunition?" Gideon called out.

"I'm out," Ian said.

"Half a clip," Brusilov replied.

Charvey clicked his trigger on an empty chamber.

"Damn," Gideon said. He gnawed his lower lip for a moment, then said, "Well, we can't take László's armed guards head on. They'll be especially alert as the train starts to pull out."

"What about the locomotive?" Charvey asked. "We can probably all squeeze in that small cab. And flashing iron should be enough to convince the engineer and fireman to do what we want them to do."

As Gideon pondered, he thought he could hear the sound of cars screeching to a halt from behind the knoll, where they had parked the bus.

"Okay," he said. "We'll do it Charvey's way. Now."

THEY TOOK OFF at a dead run.

They had to cross the open ground diagonally in order to reach the far warehouse, which meant being exposed longer. The platform and warehouses were dark and seemingly deserted, the only lights coming from the locomotive headlights and the shaded windows of the coaches. If the train hadn't been on the verge of pulling out, the team would have run in individually as a safety precaution. As it was, they went as a group, Gideon in front, Brusilov and In'Hout to the rear to provide cover.

They got to the warehouse without being seen. Keeping to the shadowed border beneath the overhang, they moved along and around the far corner of the building. Halting a few feet from trackside, Gideon motioned for Brusilov to give Ian his MP40, and for Ian to stay with Kinelly. With a few more rapid gestures, he indicated that In'Hout and Charvey were to head around the left side of the locomotive, while he and Brusilov took the right.

Nodding, In'Hout and Charvey dove in low crouches across the tracks, appearing only for an instant in the beams of the two headlamps before vanishing around the left blinder panel. Gideon and Brusilov, meanwhile, dashed single-file along the cinderbed between the back of the warehouse and the right flank of the locomotive. They pushed through the steam jets which hissed from the cylinder cocks, just as the engineer began creeping the locomotive forward to ease out the slack in the couplings.

Seizing a grabrail, Gideon hoisted himself up to the cabin, Brusilov immediately behind on the iron steps.

Startled, the engineer and fireman both gaped, the engineer with his hand on the throttle lever, the fireman stooped in the act of tossing a shovelful of coal into the firebox. Then the engineer, a swarthy older man, began barking gruffly, as though the intruders were grease monkeys from the nearby yard shops, drunk and bent on mischief. He was interrupted by Charvey and In'Hout barging in from the other side. The sight of In'Hout's MP40 instantly deflated his crusty temper.

But outrage swelled the broad pockmarked face of the fireman. When he tried to swing his coal shovel at In'Hout, Brusilov's hand shot out, grabbing the fireman by the throat of his Hungarian National Railway uniform and slamming him up hard against the cab storm window, almost shattering its oval glass. Gideon held the blade of his straight razor an inch in front of the pinned fireman's face, then looked at the engineer and held up five fingers. He started counting, folding down one finger as he recited each number.

Despite the language gap, the engineer got the message. He gulped, his hand trembling as he started levering open the throttle again. The big drivers rolled, couplers clanging and drawbars grating mechanically as the locomotive drew out the rest of the slack in the line of cars and began inching forward.

Brusilov released his grip, and the fireman tumbled to the firing deck, gasping for air. Brusilov thrust the shovel back at him, scowling. The fireman snatched up the shovel and began tossing coal from the tender through the open fire door, nodding frantically as he stoked.

At first, the train's motion was almost imperceptible. Ian and Kinelly hurried alongside, and with a helping hand from In'Hout, Kinelly was hoisted into the crowded engine compartment. Ian followed, almost losing the MP40 as he squeezed in by the tender.

The cab board and firing deck were packed and stifling, the fireman jostled every time he slung coal into the roaring firebox. Gideon stood with his spine mashed against the armrest of the side window. Yet despite feeling

116

cramped and roasted, he was drawing his first relaxed breath—when a bullet flashed through the open window an inch from his head. He ducked, peering out from around the knee of the cab.

Six or seven brownshirts were racing along the siding and platform, flame spitting from their weapons. A slug caromed off the funnel stack of the locomotive; another punched a slit in the boiler jacket by the safety-valve dome. The train was quickening now, passing the end of the warehouse and snaking through a rattling switching point onto a main rail. Still brownshirts raced after it. Suddenly, answering fire came from the observation deck at the end of the last coach. László's bodyguards, Gideon figured, assuming the count was the brownshirts' target. A bit of good luck—at just the right time.

The brownshirts sought cover as their fire was returned. The frightened engineer adjusted his bar and fed more steam to the pistons. The train gradually built speed, clattering through a succession of switches to link into the right-of-way out of Debrecen. The firing slowed, then stopped altogether as the train pulled out of range.

Gideon breathed a sigh of relief. He called Charvey to him. "Where do you think we are going?" he asked.

"I studied the timetables and route maps carefully on our trip to Miskolc. I would be very surprised if we did not head southwest to Szeged, just a few kilometers from the border into Yugoslavia."

"How long a trip is that?"

"Two hundred kilometers as the crow flies. How much longer in actuality depends on the exact route the train takes. If I could question the engineer, I could tell you how much time. But, alas—"

"We'll ask László," Gideon said with determination. "First, we have to take care of his guards. I want to give them a little time to relax after that flurry at the station. But we can't afford to wait until we reach a station where someone may have telegraphed news of our escape."

"The first such junction should be Püspökladány. About thirty-five kilometers."

Gideon pursed his lips. "I guess we have to do it now," he said. "And we want to do it quietly. No shooting,

117

unless it's absolutely the last resort. We can't afford a shootout that results in a long stalemate."

"I am ready," Brusilov said, rubbing his hands.

"No," Gideon replied. "In'Hout and Ian are better suited for climbing up over the cars. I'll go along. You stay here with Charvey and Kinelly. Keep a close watch on our two friends here."

"With pleasure," Brusilov said.

"Just a moment," In'Hout said. He pointed to the fireman's sweaty neckerchief. "To kill silently, I need that."

The fireman hesitated. Brusilov glowered at him again, and the man hastily untied the knot and handed it over.

In'Hout placed a large lump of coal in the center of the square cloth, then wound it tight. "There," he said with satisfaction, testing the slender, spiraled piece of cloth weighted by coal. "I'm ready."

Gideon motioned, and Ian and In'Hout followed as he clawed his way to the rear of the tender. From its coupler bracket, they jumped across to grab the end ladder of the baggage car, climbing up and then sprinting in a crouch along the roof plankway to the other end.

They paused, legs flexing as they gauged the sway of the train, before leaping onto László's fancy carriage. They eased along its roof plank on their bellies, not wanting to risk the noise of bootsteps reverberating down inside. Their hands tightened on bracket rungs while they swung over the top of the passenger coach—the rolling stock of this special train being the antique type, with no accordion portal to connect the cars.

Again they slid along the roof plank, cold numbing their fingers, wind whipping as if to rip them off, whiffs of engine smoke swirling in eddies around them. Faint snatches of conversation filtered up through a couple of vent pipes, but otherwise no sound came from below.

At last they reached the overhang above the observation deck. They waited a moment, then In'Hout crawled out on his side of the overhang and peered around its edge. He quickly ducked back, mouthing to the others that a guard was standing on the deck. They waited some more. Finally the glow of a cigarette butt sailed off the deck, and a minute later came the sound of a door opening and closing. In'Hout looked again, nodded, and crept to the deck's end ladder to descend on tiptoe.

From above, Gideon and Ian saw In'Hout twist from the ladder and drop silently to the observation deck. He took one cautious step, then spotted a shadow through the square window of the deck door. He pivoted to one side and flattened himself against the coach wall.

The door opened again and another guard walked out from the vestibule, carrying a bottle of beer. He was closing the door with his free hand when In'Hout came out from behind him. With a swift, dexterous motion, In'Hout looped the kerchief around the guard's neck, so that the covered lump of coal smashed squarely against the man's larynx.

The guard's body jerked as In'Hout yanked the kerchief tight. The faintest gurgle came from his shattered throat, and as he brought his hands up, In'Hout grabbed his beer bottle. In'Hout's right hand spun the kerchief tighter. For a moment, the two men stood motionless, In'Hout half crouching to support the guard's weight as his body sagged more. Finally, the arms of the guard fell and were still.

In'Hout bent down, using his body as a lever to lower the inert form to the deck. He threw the beer bottle out into the surrounding darkness and disengaged the kerchief from the dead man's throat. Then, after a quick glance toward the door, he signaled for Gideon and Ian to climb down.

Joining In'Hout, they saw the guard's eyes were wide, and blood trickled from his parted lips, staining his white coat. In'Hout started to lift the body to toss it over the deck railing.

"Wait," Gideon whispered. "He's got a pistol, and maybe some papers, a passport or something, that we can use."

"Good idea," In'Hout said. He propped the body against the coach wall, then swiftly searched through the pockets.

Again, Gideon shook his head. "Save that for later," he said. "Leave him here."

Ian rose, grinning, a thick clasp-bladed pocket knife in his hand.

They quietly opened the door. Nobody was in the vestibule, but it was impossible to see beyond its corner, down the narrow coach-long corridor connecting the compartments.

Gideon was about to start down the corridor when he heard footsteps. He waved Ian and In'Hout back out on the observation deck, closed the door, then ducked out of sight into a darkened compartment.

Gideon heard the steps halt at the door to the observation deck. "György?" a voice called. "György?"

The man opened the door. For a moment he stood in stunned amazement as he saw Ian and In'Hout. Then Gideon came up behind him, locked his arm around the guard's throat, and brought his knee viciously into his back. The guard's feet flew out from under him, and his hands clawed at Gideon's throttling arm. Ian flashed forward and sank the blade of the claspknife into the guard's chest, piercing the heart.

Ian had to tug hard to retrieve the knife. He avoided looking as Gideon rolled the second dead guard over beside the first. He was unused to knife fighting, and a slight wave of nausea shivered through him when he glimpsed the red fluid dripping off his blade. It only lasted a second. Then he wiped the knife clean on the guard's white tunic.

Again Gideon glided into the vestibule. Ian and In'Hout slipped in behind him. He shot a quick glance around the corner into the compartment corridor.

Two more white-tunicked men were standing in the corridor, their outlines highlighted by the glow coming from a compartment halfway down the car. They were talking, one chuckling as though at a joke. Then, still chuckling, he returned to the compartment and slide its door closed. The other man started walking toward László's coach.

"Let's get him back here," Gideon whispered. He darted around the corner, into the first compartment. It was empty, its lights off and curtains drawn across its corridor windows. Gideon eased the door half closed, drawing one curtain with it, then stood waiting behind it, hidden from the dim corridor light.

Unseen around the corner, In'Hout made a retching noise.

The man in the corridor stopped.

In'Hout coughed again, being careful not to sound too ill. Otherwise the man might summon help.

The curious man started back along the corridor. Closer and closer came his steps, until his right shoulder and arm brushed against the compartment door. To Gideon's surprise and intense pleasure, he recognized the man—Vilém. He tensed, poised for the traitor to pass by.

Instead, Vilém glanced toward the open doorway, scanning from habit. He caught a glimpse of Gideon's hovering form. His step faltered, though his pace carried him another foot before he could stop. By then, Gideon was moving.

His eyes full of terror, Vilém tried to scream, but fright closed his throat. He stumbled back a step away from Gideon, and one of his hands started to rise in a defensive reflex. But it was too late to prevent the lightning-quick razor slash. Vilém's hand kept rising, touching the throat that had been slashed from ear to ear, feeling the blood that spurted.

Vilém sagged, his hand still at his neck. His knees buckled, and as Gideon swiftly opened the compartment door all the way, he toppled face down onto the floor. Gideon pushed him completely inside, drew the curtain fully closed, and shut the door.

"We paid that bastard back," Gideon said. "Now let's finish off the others."

In'Hout and Ian came out from the vestibule, and the three began gliding down the corridor, checking each compartment as they went. Most were dark; all were empty.

They paused midway, where Vilém's chuckling subordinate had entered a compartment. They could hear subdued voices from within, and another sound like the clinking of bottles. Gideon edged to the other side of the compartment door, then crouched, leaning so he could grab the handle without being seen. He wrenched back the door, and In'Hout and Ian leaped inside. Gideon was up and rushing right beside them.

The last two guards were sitting by the coach window, facing each other across a folded-down snack table. They reared, fumbling for their Lugers, their movements hampered by the table.

Ian dove for the man on the left. His knife bored low into the man's throat by the breastbone. There was a gurgling hiss like air drawing from a pipe, and together they tumbled across the worn green plush seat. Ian stabbed again, then a third time. The guard's face contorted with agony, then his head tilted to one side as he died.

In'Hout had launched himself at the other guard, tackling him before the man could get out from behind the table. His hand clawed into the man's crotch, grappling for his scrotum and twisting it viciously. The guard screamed as he struggled to break In'Hout's grip. But In'Hout punched the guard with his free hand. The guard gagged on broken teeth. In'Hout forced his head back, increasing the pressure until something snapped. The guard went limp.

"Get their pistols," Gideon ordered.

Quickly the corpses were stripped of their Lugers. The compartment lights were switched off, the curtains drawn, and the three returned to the corridor.

The rest of the coach proved to be empty.

Reaching the front vestibule, the team glanced back along the corridor. The only signs of their deadly passage were the ruby puddle outside the first compartment, where Vilém had paid for his betrayal, and the red-stained footprints they'd tracked from the compartment where they'd slain the last two guards.

Ahead lay Count László's private carriage. And a conversation Gideon very much looked forward to.

13

JUMPING THE COUPLERS, they stood swaying for a moment on the narrow ledge outside the exit door of Count László's private coach.

Gideon said to Ian and In'Hout, "Keep your weapons ready. But don't be too anxious to use them. We need László alive."

They nodded.

Gideon led the way through the door and the rear vestibule. The corridor went only halfway up the carriage. Flanking it were four large sleeping compartments, all of which were empty.

At the end of the corridor was a carved mahogany door with a frosted glass window. Through the door they could hear the strains of a symphony mixed with snatches of conversation.

Gideon quietly turned the handle of the door and pushed.

Count László was sitting in a wing-tip armchair, his burgundy smoking jacket unbuttoned, his outstretched right hand holding a long-stemmed wineglass. When he saw Gideon, a look of astonishment swept over his face. The wineglass fell, smashing on the carpet.

Eliska stood by László's extended arm, slowly righting the bottle of white wine she was about to pour. She wore a shiny royal-blue satin dress that highlighted the gentle curves of her lithe body.

Eliska spoke first. "Scott," she said with a huge smile,

"thank God you're all right. We were so worried about you."

Gideon's face was a stern mask, hiding his emotions. "You were worried? Your Count László here knew exactly where we were. Or, rather, where he hoped we were."

A look of deep puzzlement settled over Eliska's face. "What are talking about?" she asked. "The count sent out men to look for you. He—"

"I bet he did," Gideon said, staring hard at the pale and visibly trembling László. He shifted his gaze back to Eliska. "Let me explain. Vilém led us to the warehouse to dump off the trucks. Then he served us up on a silver platter to a dozen armed brownshirts."

Eliska's mouth dropped open. She was too stunned to utter a word.

"Vilém is a traitor," László said. "I should have known." The count had recovered his aristocratic demeanor, and he spoke with a convincing tone of authority. "There have been so many unexplained occurrences. Now I understand. Vilém has fooled us all. I shall see that he pays harshly."

"He can't pay any more harshly than he did a few minutes ago," In'Hout said.

"You mean he is dead?" László asked. "Good, then. He deserves his fate. His disservice to his country is—"

"Cut the shit, László," Gideon snapped. "It's not going to work. We had a very interesting chat with your buddy Gyul Dánya. Your game is over."

László stood, stone-faced, staring at Gideon.

"What game?" Eliska asked, looking back and forth between the two grim-faced men.

Gideon turned to her. "I'll make it very simple. This guy Dánya is—or rather," he interjected, throwing a glance at László, "was, a big shot in the Arrow Front. He told us that László is secretly a member of the party. The proceeds from the sale of the treasure are to be used not for weapons for the resistance, but to set up an espionage network in foreign capitals."

"Rubbish," László scoffed.

"I don't believe it," Eliska said.

"I don't either," Gideon replied. "I don't think László

was any more honest with the Fascists than he was with us. I think his intention was to play everyone for fools. Not for a moment was a single piece of the László treasure going to be sold for any purpose, much less for arms for the resistance. The treasure would remain intact, while László sold the possessions of his fellow aristocrats to support himself in lavish fashion in whichever safe corner of the world he decided to sit out the war."

"Lies," László insisted. "All lies." He looked at Eliska. "It is true that I arranged for these men to be detained. I discovered that they were nothing more than bandits, who planned to seize the precious wealth of our homeland for their own personal gain."

Eliska was white-faced and trembling, but her voice was firm. She looked directly into László's eyes and said, "Of all the things that have been said, the one which I am certain is not true is that Gideon and his men are bandits. Some say that in war a man's true heart is revealed. I have traveled with these men and fought with them, and I believe that they are what they say they are."

László's lips curled into an expression of contempt as he spoke to her. "So you are like the rest. With your intelligence, I had hopes for you. Now I see all too clearly that you are exactly like your father and brother, pathetic fools, sucking on the outmoded tit of patriotism."

A shock went through Eliska as she recoiled from László's verbal assault. She gaped at him, shaking her head, saying, "No, no, you can't mean that."

Then she moved to him, grabbing the left sleeve of his smoking jacket with both hands. "Zsigmond," she pleaded, "say that you don't mean that. Not for the sake of the love we shared, but for the dreams we shared for our homeland."

"Our homeland is full of sheep, peasants clinging to barren rocks. Hitler has proved that the modern age is the age of wolves. One is either a predator or a slave, and no László has ever been a slave."

"Your days as a wolf are over, László," Gideon said. "You'd better get used to—"

In a quick move, László grabbed Eliska around the throat and pulled her in front of him. At the same time, his right hand snaked into his jacket pocket and emerged with an eight-shot Mauser .25 WTP automatic.

"Drop your weapons," László commanded.

Gideon smiled. "Forget it, László. There's no way out of this corner. Vilém and your four bodyguards are dead. I have three men in the locomotive. You can't drag her with you over the tender, and you're no match for an MP40 with that popgun in your right hand."

"You'll stop this train to let me off," László said, his face red and his eyes reflecting panic for the first time.

Gideon ignored his words. "I'll tell you one thing. If you should be so foolish as to harm Eliska in any way, your death won't be quick. You'll die the slowest, most horrible death whichever of us are left can dream up. And we have pretty lively imaginations."

László's gun hand was shaking. He took a deep breath. Then the fight seemed to go out of him. Resignation replaced the last shred of hope on his face. His gun hand dropped to his side as he released Eliska.

"Good decision, László," Gideon said. "You cooperate with us the rest of the trip, and we'll see you're treated leniently wherever we end up. We're not bandits, as Eliska pointed out. We'll stick to our end of the bargain and let you keep your share of your treasures."

As pale as he was, László retained some of his arrogance. "You think you have conquered me totally," he said. "But that is not true. In all the centuries of our history, no head of the house of László has bowed before another man. I, too, refuse to bow."

What László planned suddenly flashed into Gideon's mind. He started forward.

László was quicker. He raised the Mauser to his temple and pulled the trigger. The explosion was shockingly loud in the confines of the salon.

Eliska collapsed, sobbing, into a chair. Gideon moved to comfort her while In'Hout knelt by László.

"He's dead," In'Hout announced.

Eliska clung to Gideon. Finally her trembling subsided. Gideon dropped his arms as she took out a handkerchief and wiped her eyes and nose.

When she looked up at him, her eyes were full of

sadness. "It has ended for me," she said. "First my parents, then my brother taken from me. All I had left to believe in was Count László and what he stood for. Now my life is over. There is nowhere I belong."

"That isn't true," Gideon said. "You suffered tragedies. But Ian's entire family was murdered by the Nazis in Poland. Brusilov's country was seized by the Bolsheviks. In'Hout and his fellow Jews have become hunted outcasts. All of us, in our own ways, are exiles. But we have found a cause that brings us together in a powerful bond —Phoenix, a symbol of resistance." He paused for a moment, looking her directly in the eyes. "I think I speak for the team in saying that we'd like you to join us."

Eliska stared at him in surprise.

"You've proved yourself to me," Gideon said. "What about you?" He turned to face Ian and In'Hout.

Ian, smiling, said, "It's fine by me."

"I'd trust her with my life," In'Hout said. "Besides, I need someone to look at besides Kinelly."

Joy suffused Eliska's face. She hugged Gideon, then rose and embraced Ian and In'Hout in turn.

Gideon savored the emotion of the moment along with the rest of the team. It was true, he thought, what Eliska had said about a man's heart being revealed in war. It was also true of a woman's heart and courage. Eliska had amply demonstrated that she was an equal of any member of Phoenix.

Finally, Gideon said, "We'd better get going. Let's get out of Hungary before we celebrate too much."

"I know where the paperwork is," Eliska said. "The travel permits, and the entry papers for the crossing into Yugoslavia."

"Entry into Yugoslavia is the least of our immediate problems," Gideon said. "And I don't think those travel papers are going to do us any good. When we blasted our way out of that brownshirt headquarters, we probably queered the whole deal László had arranged. I'm sure the alert has gone out for us. Maybe we have enough of a head start to get all the way to the border. Or maybe, somebody's preparing an unpleasant surprise for us up ahead."

"Any idea where that might happen?" Ian asked.

"No," Gideon said. He asked Eliska, "Do you know the route?"

"I'm afraid not."

"Then we'll have to find those papers. Eliska, you'll have to come up to the locomotive with me to act as interpreter so Charvey can grill the engineer. We'll have to depend on Charvey,"

"Let's go," Eliska said.

Gideon pointed to her clothes and said, "I think you'd better change into something a little more suitable for action. I mean," he added, "the kind of action we're likely to see."

She smiled briefly and hurried to her compartment. Gideon said to Ian and In'Hout, "I want you to search the car behind us and this car. I want any relevant papers and maps. Second, gather up all the valuables—money, jewels, gold—so we can store that in the baggage car. And finally, scrounge up all the weapons and ammo you can."

"So you think the chances are we'll have to fight our way through?" In'Hout asked.

Gideon grimaced. "I don't think this is going to be a relaxing ride."

14

GIDEON AND ELISKA made their way through the packed baggage car. When they exited and started to climb over the tender, Gideon was suddenly aware how cold it was. The night wind off the flat plain combined with the speed of the locomotive blasted frigidly against his face, numbing skin and narrowing his eyelid to slits. He was grateful for the heat when he jumped to the firing deck.

Kinelly was sitting on the fireman's bench, Brusilov leaning against the door, and Charvey standing next to the engineer, whose hand was resting on the throttle bar while he stared out the cab's storm window at the track ahead.

Brusilov moved toward them. "László?" he asked expectantly.

"Dead," Gideon said. "I'll tell you the story later. Right now I brought Eliska to find out from the engineer where the hell he's taking us."

Charvey turned. "He's not taking us anywhere. That is, he only makes the train stop and start. The direction is prescheduled."

"I think that schedule may be changed," Gideon said. "But at least we can start with an idea of where we're supposed to be going. Eliska?"

As she moved forward and started quizzing the engineer in Hungarian, Charvey asked Gideon, "What is your plan?"

"I don't know. All I do know is that we've got to be out of Hungary by dawn. That gives us five hours."

"By train, that should be ample time," Charvey said.

"If we don't run into trouble. But whizzing along on this track I feel like a sitting duck."

Eliska finished her questioning and moved back to join them. "The engineer said we will be on the main line until Szolnok, then south to Békéscsaba and on to Szeged."

"How far is Szolnok from here?"

Charvey answered. "From the route map I looked at, I think it is perhaps a hundred kilometers from Debrecen. And less than a hundred kilometers from Budapest."

Gideon frowned. "The last thing we want to do is get anywhere near Budapest. What about branch lines?"

"There are numerous cutoffs and branch lines," Charvey said. "But they present a problem. Almost all of them are single-track. If we should meet another train coming the other way, well . . ." He shrugged expressively.

"I get the message," Gideon said.

"But there is a way," Charvey said. "That is to study the schedule in depth to work out a clear path. Even then, there is the risk of a disabled train. But at least it is a chance."

"Are there schedules on this train?"

Eliska asked the engineer, who responded with an emphatic negative that didn't need translation. After another brief exchange, Eliska told Gideon, "The detailed timetables can be obtained only at the more major stations. The next is Püspökladány, which we shall reach soon."

Gideon turned to stand by the door. They were chugging away through the dimly moonlit Alföld, with only the paralleling rail lines of the right-of-way, briefly illuminated by the locomotive's headlights, cutting across the expanse of flat, bleak plain.

As Gideon stared, he worked on focusing his mind on reviewing the situation and the alternatives clearly and logically. It wasn't easy. Gideon had found that far more than physical prowess, courage, or charisma, the ability to think clearly under the intense emotional and physical stress of combat was his most difficult challenge as a leader of men in war.

The pressure could hardly get any higher than on this mission. They were six men and a woman hurtling through an unknown land with ten million dollars' worth of art, their lives and those of countless future resistance fighters dependent on escaping the entire forces of the Hungarian army, air force, and local police.

Gideon was so weary and lost in thought that he almost lost his balance as the train rounded a sweeping curve. He caught himself, then leaned his head out, letting the ice-cold air slap his face. He had to force his mind back to work.

He began. Option One: continuing on the course laid out by László. From a practical standpoint, the easiest. The fastest way to Yugoslavia, if all went right. That was the joker in the deck. He'd been nervous about the quality of the safe-conduct László had bought even before their own shocking betrayal. His confidence that the plan would work after their very public escape in Debrecen was practically nil.

Option Two: find a couple trucks, transfer the cargo, and flee by road. Assuming that they could get suitable vehicles—a large assumption—this alternative had the sizable practical advantage of making pursuit or interception a lot more difficult. There would be ten alternatives in a motor vehicle for every branch line or cutoff available to a train.

The problem was efficiency. First, the time necessary to transfer the art. And second, the team's exhaustion. Gideon had enough experience with the horrendous Hungarian roads to know that hours of driving in their present condition might simply be too much.

That left Option Three: using branch lines to zigzag their way south to the border. The chances of trouble were great, but better, he thought intuitively, than staying with László's predetermined route. Besides, remaining on the train allowed the Phoenix team to save their energy for fighting. And that, to Gideon's mind, was the decisive factor. If they were going down, it was going to be with barrels blazing and a lot of enemy falling around them.

He exhaled, then stuck his head out for another bracing blast of air. Then he turned back into the cab and said to Charvey and Eliska, "We're going to try the branch lines."

The others nodded silently. Gideon was their leader; the crucial decision was his to make.

Soon the outskirts of Püspökladány began flicking past on their left. The rear plots of houses and sheds grew thicker together, the grade crossings more numerous. It reminded Gideon of an American whistle stop, flanked by tracks on one side and by a highway on the other.

About a kilometer past a major grade crossing, the engineer started easing on the bar while he applied the brakes, gradually slowing the train.

"Tell him to stop before we get to the station," Gideon said to Eliska.

"No need," Charvey said. "Look ahead."

When Gideon looked, he saw the red eye of a signal looming against the darkness.

"Red," Gideon said with alarm. "That might mean a trap. Marcel, can we go on?"

"No, no," Charvey answered quickly. "If we try to go through, the signal will derail us. Besides, the red light only indicates that the track ahead is not safe. It could mean an open switch, a train dead on the track, or ten other things."

"I still don't like it," Gideon said. "Tell the engineer to stop here. Now!"

Eliska relayed the sharp command. The engineer jammed the throttle bar closed and fixed the brakes, locking the shoes against the drivers. Shuddering, the locomotive grated into a long skid, sending out a metallic shriek and a shower of sparks. It ground to a halt, boiler panting hotly, headlamps reflecting off the station platform fifty yards distant.

The night seemed suddenly still. The team members stared out the left side of the cab at the station, a black outline against the moonlit sky. As was typical in Hungary, the station was huge, a two-story structure topped by a round cupola. The building was made more imposing by the fact that it sat alone, without any other buildings nearby to challenge its solitary hegemony over the steel rails below.

Something about the scene gave Gideon an eerie feeling, and he wished he'd had a chance to go back to the rear coaches to see what weapons Ian and In'Hout had managed to round up. They were going to be out-gunned if—

He spun as he heard a sound behind him. The fireman had taken their preoccupation with the building as an opportunity to flee. He leaped out the right side of the cab and started running toward the station. Gideon took a step after him.

Then a machine gun opened up. The fireman clutched his chest as a stitch of machine-gun bullets hit him. He stumbled a step or two, then his body flopped on the trackside bed.

"Down!" Gideon shouted, pulling Eliska with him to the cab board. More gunfire erupted. The storm window of the locomotive shattered and the engineer, slow to realize what was happening, fell on his back, a gurgling hole opened in his chest.

More lead whanged against the cab and the sides of the cars, breaking glass and ricocheting through the darkness. Gideon moved across to the right side, leaving Brusilov and Charvey facing the station side. Then they began blazing back at the firepoints of the attackers. Ian and In'Hout had set up a rear defensive position, and Gideon heard heavy fire pouring out from the passenger coach.

Gideon's pistol clicked empty. "I've got to get more weapons and ammo," he yelled.

He dove from the cab in a twist that flung his body at an angle, away from the burst of rifle fire opening up on him. Doubling to his hands and knees, he rolled under the tender and began creeping swiftly between the rails toward the passenger coach.

For the first time, he got a glimpse of their attackers. From the grassy slope bordering the track a line of brownshirts fired continuously. The wheel trucks and rails sang with the impact of their slugs. An erratic fusilade followed Gideon's progress back to the end of the train. He crawled as fast as he could, the framing and equipment of the cars' undercarriages keeping him low to the cinders. As the shots nipped around him, he tried both to count his attackers and track their movements.

Reaching the observation deck at the rear, he lay under its coupler brackets and called urgently, "Toss me a pistol."

In'Hout answered. "Here's an MP40."

"Great," Gideon said, snatching the machine pistol when it dropped in front of him. "We've got to mow right up the line. There must be a dozen men broadsiding us out here. I can't tell how many more are holed up in the station."

"We'll take them," In'Hout said confidently. "That sniper up in the station's cupola, though, could be real trouble. He can get the drop on all of us."

With that, In'Hout vaulted over the left rail of the observation deck, his MP40 cutting accurately through two onrushing brownshirts as he sprinted crouching toward the station.

Gideon scrambled from underneath the coupler, angling back along the right side with lead spanking about him. He heard In'Hout yelling to Ian, when Ian swung from the salon exit to join him, but it was impossible to hear either one of them after that, with the sharp blasts spurting from the slope as the pair loped forward, spraying everything before them.

Gideon moved slower along his side of the train, ducking in and out of cover so he could aim at the flashing winks of enemy weapons. The machine pistol bucked hot in his grip, its savage reports ringing in his ears. Gradually, the volume of fire snarling about him lessened.

Then, as Gideon came up alongside the locomotive once again, a silence fell, the fire fight suddenly evaporating. He heard the sound of men scrambling over the tracks in the darkness. That would be the few remaining brownshirts retreating to the station, he guessed.

Charvey slipped out of the train beside him. Brusilov stayed in the locomotive, selectively returning fire as sporadic shots flew from the station.

"We are pinned down here," Charvey said. "We couldn't use grenades even if we had them. We couldn't risk destroying the route board and the schedules."

"Well, we've only got one choice," Gideon said. "We've got to get you inside that station." He called to Ian, sending him back to the coaches to pick up additional weapons and ammunition. When Ian returned, Gideon crawled into the cab and handed machine pistols to Eliska and Kinelly, and gave additional clips to Brusilov.

"You three are going to lay down covering fire for us," he said. "We're going to make a run for it."

Gideon dropped back down out of the locomotive, then crouched by the engine truck wheel and told Charvey, "You and I will go first. Ian and Joel will follow."

Gideon took a deep breath, steadying his nerves. He knew Charvey was tensed and ready to move beside him. Then the two charged.

They raced zigzagging across the tracks. A brownshirt appeared in the station doorway with a machine gun in his hands, but an instant later he reeled and fell over the edge of the platform, a victim of the intense volume of fire pouring from the locomotive.

Despite the covering fire, the brownshirts in the station weren't silent. A bullet gouged the heel of Gideon's right boot, and another whined uncomfortably close to his head. Gideon spun to his right, then, twisting and turning like a halfback in the open field, bolted the twenty remaining yards to the station.

He reached the edge of the building safely, and seconds later Charvey slid to a stop beside him.

They took a quick moment to catch their breath before sliding along the plank wall of the building, keeping flat against it so the roof's overhang would protect them from the sniper above. There they waited nervously while Ian and In'Hout negotiated the same perilous gauntlet to the station, then joined them by the rear corner.

The four edged around the street side of the station. The waiting-room entrance was in the middle of the building; shuttered windows were on one side, and on the other was a large overhead door for freight shipments. The team eased toward the wooden door of the entrance, hunching to stay below the wide sills of the windows.

A shutter above Ian banged open. A man leaned out,

angling downward as he fired an old carbine. Ian shot straight up. The man clawed at his brown shirt, and with a single groan slumped out of sight. The unshuttered window spat out bullets from the remaining brownshirts inside.

Gideon and Charvey hit the wooden door together, dashing in and swiveling to each side, drenching the waiting room in a hail of lead. A brownshirt vanished behind a ticket-window counter, his rifle clattering to the floor. Charvey laced another who was hiding under a desk, the man squeezing off a round as he collapsed, a puff of dust marking the spot where his bullet entered the wooden wainscot. Huddled against the staircase leading to the cupola was a third brownshirt, already wounded, his eyes glaring from the crimson mask of his face as he trained his pistol on Gideon. Gideon dropped him, their two shots roaring simultaneously.

"You look for the schedules and whatever else you need," Gideon called to Charvey. "We'll go for that sniper."

He led the way to the base of the wooden staircase, which had a twist in it halfway to the second floor. Gideon climbed cautiously to that point. He stuck his head out for a look, then quickly snapped it back as a burst of fire poured down from above.

Gideon realized the situation was a stalemate. They couldn't be hit directly from above, and ricochets were virtually eliminated by the soft old plaster walls that soaked up the bullets like a sponge. But they couldn't climb higher, either; the enemy's line of fire was impossible to challenge.

Gideon glanced back down over the railing. Below, the station interior swirled with smoke, the strangely repugnant odor of blood, powder, dry rot, and stale tobacco reaching his nose. His gaze moved to the far end of the interior, where he noticed a long bank of cogwheel levers used for manipulating switch points and signals. At its far end, Charvey was studying a large system map of the entire railway mounted on a board underneath a green-shaded wall lamp. Beyond Charvey came the impatient clicking of an unattended telegraph.

Gideon jerked his head back toward the stairway, puzzled by the sudden burst of firing from above. The answer to the puzzle was provided when Brusilov chugged through the door into the station.

Brusilov approached Gideon, a look of urgency on his broad face. "We have to get out of here. Lights are on everywhere, and we're pinned down on that train. And down the highway from Debrecen, I saw the headlights of what looks to be a convoy of trucks."

"We've got a problem upstairs," Gideon said. "We can't get past this corner."

Brusilov studied the situation for a moment. "Perhaps," he suggested with a smile, "you forget a basic rule, my friend. Fight fire with fire."

"I don't understand," Gideon said impatiently.

"Wait," Brusilov replied. He hurried across the waiting room and barked a question at Charvey. The two of them disappeared into the stationmaster's office. Brusilov emerged carrying a kerosene signal lantern in each hand.

Now Gideon understood. "Terrific," he said, nodding his head.

Brusilov handed his weapon to Gideon. Then he lit the wick of a lantern, stood, and flung it up around the twist in the stairs. An instant later they heard a loud whoosh as the lantern exploded, followed by an agonized scream.

Gideon led the charge up the stairs, raking the area above him with withering automatic fire. He heard two more screams from behind the wall of flames.

Gideon stopped and turned back to Brusilov. "How about the cupola?"

Brusilov stepped forward. Through the fire and smoke a wooden ladder led up to a trapdoor to the roof. He lit the second lantern, and with a mighty heave crashed it against the base of the ladder, where it exploded.

The flames quickly raced up the dry wood and licked at the trapdoor. Brusilov grabbed his machine pistol and blasted at the door. The bullets shredded the thin wood, creating a draft for the fire.

Brusilov said to Gideon, "That will keep our last remaining friend busy. Let's get out of here before we are roasted."

137

They sprinted back down the stairs, out of the station, and across the fifty yards to the train.

"Get the rear of the train again," Gideon shouted to Ian and In'Hout. He jumped in the locomotive. The high scream of sirens was drawing closer; they had almost no time left.

Gideon looked around, registering the tense, anxious faces of Eliska, Kinelly, and Brusilov. Then he realized Charvey was missing. A jolt of panic went through him. If something had happened to Charvey, they were lost.

"Where's Marcel?" he shouted. When they had no answer, Gideon instantly turned his attention to the controls of the locomotive. The front of the cab was a maze of gauges and valves and levers. But there was no time left. The only thing he recognized was the throttle bar. He reached for it, jerking the lever a couple notches down its quadrant.

The locomotive shuddered violently as the drive wheels responded to the abrupt surge of steam in the cylinders. But the torque was overpowering, and the wheels spun on the rails without getting traction, the drive rods thrashing impotently. Realizing his error, Gideon hastily backed off the throttle.

"What're you doing?" Charvey yelled, hoisting himself into the cab. "Stop fooling around before you ruin my engine."

Gideon allowed himself a thin, tight smile. He couldn't remember being happier to see anyone in his life.

With practiced ease, Charvey released the brake, notched the reverse bar, and pulled open the throttle. "I teethed on old crocks like this," he said with pride.

The locomotive chugged, hissed, and started rolling past the station, bumping slightly as the wheels sliced through a brownshirt who'd been lying dead across one rail. Gideon slumped onto the fireman's bench, exhaling with relief. Then he remembered the red signal light.

"Hey, we can't . . ." he began. Then he felt the squeaking jar of switch points, the locomotive angling from the main line, curving left on another track. He said to Charvey, "What are we on? A siding?"

"A branch line south. But I couldn't be sure I'd thrown

the correct levers without checking." Charvey tapped the corner of one eye. "That's where I've been, looking over the switches."

"Good. Then let's get on with it."

But instead, Charvey throttled back and braked. The train ground to a halt again, the tender directly under the dark bulk of a water tower. "Fill the tank in the tender," Charvey shouted.

"How?" Gideon shouted. Then he shouted louder as Marcel showed no signs of having heard, "Come back here."

But Charvey had already dropped from the cab and was racing toward the station as though he'd forgotten something there.

Gideon clambered up over the coal. The rear section of the tender was one huge square tank, with two large lids on top. He had no idea how to fill it, his only knowledge of tenders being vague childhood memories from western movies. He opened both lids on the tender tank, then reached high to grab the rope dangling from the water-tower pipe. The pipe hinged down, releasing a torrent on him before he could center its gooseneck spigot in one of the tank's openings.

Sirens were now sounding shrill in his ears. Above them, he suddenly heard the staccato fire of an MP40 echoing from inside the station, and at first he feared Charvey had run into trouble.

He peered around the side of the tender and spotted uniformed Hungarians tumbling from a truck in front of the station. He released the water pipe, drenching himself again while he kicked the lids shut. He was about to leap off the tender to help when he glimpsed Charvey darting up along the coaches.

A bullet clipped past Gideon's ear. He dove over the coal, landing on the firing deck, just as Charvey pulled himself inside and sprang to push the throttle forward. The willing driver wheels took hold as steam poured against the pistons. More bullets whined through the cab. Charvey, seemingly oblivious to the shots, stood calmly in front of the boiler head, examining the dials.

"Pressure's still low," he remarked blandly, as though they were on a picnic. "You want to ride as fireman?"

"Yeah, yeah, only let's get riding."

Charvey reached down and opened the door of the firebox. Flames licked out, almost singeing Gideon's leg. The Frenchman pointed to the shovel lying by the coal. "Then start stoking, fireman."

Gideon snatched the handle of the shovel and started throwing coal on the fire as if his life depended on it; it did.

15

THE GUNFIRE INCREASED steadily, lead richocheting off the cab and engine with sharp, high retorts. The soldiers were smarter than the brownshirts had been, Gideon realized; they were concentrating on the boiler, trying to pierce it and immobilize the locomotive.

But the locomotive was a tough old brute, built of heavy, armor-thick steel plates. And under Charvey's able handling, it continued to pick up speed, its exhaust swelling to a rhythmic thunder, belching sulfurous clouds as it surged faster, the rolling stock behind swaying and clanking in accompaniment. Then, suddenly Püspökladány was behind them, and the train was tearing out alone across the Great Hungarian Plain, the sounds of gunfire fading away.

Charvey was paying scant attention to the track ahead. He had his back to the storm window, one arm crooked around the throttle bar for support, while he consulted the complex timetable folders.

Gideon heaved more coal in the firebox, then paused to catch his breath. He called out to Charvey, "One question. Why did you run back into the station? You almost got us killed with the delay."

"I went back to throw the switching levers back to their original positions," Charvey answered, "and then disable the levers' latch handles so they can't be moved again. Now, any train on the main line must stay on it, and can't switch onto this branch to chase us. And while I was at it, I shot up the telegraph terminal board."

A smile flashed across Charvey's face, making him look for a moment like a naughty schoolboy who had just successfully completed a prank.

Gideon nodded toward the schedules. "Do you think your plan will work?"

"It's an awkward route, but if we are lucky and careful, we've got a good chance. Right now," Charvey added, "I'm more concerned the engine doesn't blow." He glanced at the gauges. "The boiler is leaking water now."

Gideon viewed the huge mound in the tender. "Well, we won't run out of coal, at least," he said. He began shoveling coal again into the firebox billowing with raging heat.

The train flashed by the tiny depot of a tiny village, crossing from one side of a paralleling farm road to the other, then flanked it and roared toward the glow of a town ten kilometers distant. Charvey didn't let up their breakneck pace as they raced into the town, leaning on the blaring whistle instead to clear traffic at grade crossings. They entered into the station yard with such a jolting and screeching that Gideon held his breath, sure they were going to crash and overturn at any second.

"Hey," Gideon called out. "Slow down."

Charvey turned around and bellowed, "I'm trying to clear this stretch of line. It's the only one to Szeghalom from Püspökladány, and they'll know that. But going out of Szeghalom are six lines, and they won't know which one we've taken."

"Will we know?"

"According to the schedules, the last train has cleared the track from Sarkad to Szeghalom. That's not a bad direction, and in theory, the signals should still be open all the way."

Charvey turned back toward the controls. Twenty minutes later, he braked a little as they approached Szeghalom.

Szeghalom was about the same size as Püspökladány. The town seemed to be asleep, the station and the surrounding yards unlit and deserted. Gideon tensed, waiting for shots to fly. But Charvey whistled a path across three intersecting roads, navigated a web of switching points, and ended up on a track on the other side of town.

The train plunged once more into the dark reaches of the Alföld. "Are you sure we're headed the right way?" Gideon asked. The maze of tracks at Szeghalom seemed an unsolvable puzzle to him.

Charvey shrugged. "I think so, but I can't be sure until we pass the next station. Let's keep our fingers crossed."

Brusilov took over from Gideon. Sweating profusely, Gideon stepped aside and stood at the window as the train resumed its horrendous clip. After ten kilometers of straightaway, the track suddenly split into a Y, and the train automatically veered to the right, wheel flanges grating protestingly against the rails.

"Vézlö," Charvey called, reading the sign on the junction depot. "Perfect."

On the train rocketed in a long, S-curve to the southwest. After fifteen swift kilometers they approached a junction where another line crossed theirs. The intersection had feeder tracks so that trains could be shunted from one line to the other, and Charvey brought the train to a shivering halt a few yards before the first feeder-track switch.

"Give me your pistol," Charvey said to Gideon.

Gideon handed over a Luger, then went along with Charvey while he climbed down to the tracks and hastened over to the switch. In the glare of the locomotive headlight, Gideon saw that the switch was the manually operated type, with multicolored panels on top to indicate which way it was set. The panels took the place of signal lights, the feeder track being too far from a main depot to have electricity.

Charvey shot an ancient padlock off the switch, raised its lever and moved it around to another position, then ran over to the corresponding switch on the other line, did the same thing, and returned to the cab. He throttled the engine forward, along the feeder and onto the other line. When the rear wheels of the passenger coach had just scraped past the second switch, he braked again, went down and levered both switches to the way they'd first been, and came back.

"We're not going to Sarkad," he said, trying to catch his breath. "I figured out a better route. Thirty minutes, maybe less, we'll be in Békéscsaba. From there it's perhaps eighty kilometers to Szeged and the border. On more of a main line, I'm afraid, but it can't be avoided."

"Where's it go in Yugoslavia?"

"Stops at Sobotica, where László was originally headed. By a different route." Charvey grinned. "We're taking the scenic route, eh?"

Brusilov was taking a break from shoveling. He wiped the torrent of perspiration streaming down his forehead, then asked Gideon, "Have you given a thought to what will happen at the border?"

"We have László's papers and freight manifesto."

"We also have a shot-up train with stolen treasures and a trail of Hungarians after us. I do not want to end up in a Yugoslavian jail for months while they try to decide what to do with us."

"You've got a point there," Gideon said. "Let me chew on it for a while."

The trackbed ran southeast along a narrow embankment above stretches of marshy grassland. As they neared Békéscsába, the land became drier and firmer, and the tracks leveled onto it, the train whizzing by farms and outbuildings toward the town's center. In sight of the station, another line joined in on their left, but the signal was green, so Charvey continued into the trainyard.

They were rumbling past the station on the far track when Charvey braked to a shuddering halt. He said to Gideon, "We've got trouble."

Gideon looked around. Like Szeghalom, the town appeared to be peacefully slumbering. The station was dark and locked up for the night. Close by, a branch line curved toward the right, its switch closed against entry, its signal red. Some distance ahead, where the yard tracks linked together into a right-of-way heading south, a long freight train was off on a siding, chugging idly. The signal far beyond it glowed like a red firefly. Surveying the

144

tracks behind them, Gideon saw that all the signals were green.

"The signal past that freight is the trouble, right?"

"No, I expected it to be red. According to the schedules, a train should be somewhere ahead of us, going in our same direction. No trouble there. And we've made good time, considering, so it wouldn't be surprising if it was still in the section the signal controls. Once it was through, the signal would turn green, the section clear."

"Then what? Nobody's hiding around here."

"No, the station and yards are deserted."

"And the freight doesn't look like an ambush."

"No, it's merely obeying the signals."

"Okay, I'm stumped," Gideon said.

"The train we should be following is that freight," Charvey explained. "Why is it waiting? No other trains are due until morning. If the track is being repaired, at least a leverman would be on duty to direct the train on after the work crews are done. But the station is closed. I suspect the freight has been stopped because there is an incoming *unscheduled* train on the section ahead. Meaning it could arrive here any minute. Must I tell you what that means?"

Gideon gestured toward the right. "It means we turn off on that branch line there."

"*Exactement.* Now, time's too short for me to go back and forth changing switches, and the freight crew would probably notice it anyway. I'll work the switches, while you do the starting and stopping."

"Oh, no. You drive. I'll switch."

"You would not know which levers," Charvey said, climbing down and pausing on the cinders. "When the light turns green, ease on the throttle. I mean *ease* on it Gideon. When you roll past the switch, ease on the brake."

"But . . ."

Charvey, waving, angled back across the tracks toward the station. He vanished in the shadows of the platform's overhang. Gideon heard a muffled crunch of glass, then the squeak of door hinges. A minute later, the signal for the branch line flashed to green.

145

"Damn," Gideon muttered, leery after his first experience. He throttled forward with a feathery touch. The locomotive obediently crept up to the switching point and trundled through onto the branch line. The branch's signal slid back to red as Charvey reclosed the switch behind the train.

Now to stop. Gideon frantically tested various levers without locating the brake mechanism. His heart was pounding. He put the throttle bar into neutral, which only seemed to add to the speed of the crawling locomotive. He was about to take a chance and thrust the bar into reverse position when Charvey, running madly, grabbed the cab rail and scrambled aboard.

"No!" Charvey panted breathlessly, lunging to take over the controls. "Thank God. You would have torn up the engine."

Gideon gladly backed away from the controls as the locomotive again picked up speed.

The branch line they were now on was seldom traveled, the rails rusty and uneven in stretches. The train rattled and bounced as it sped southwest, then curved southeast, running alongside a rutted country road. They intersected a secondary route at a grade crossing and made a wide bend southwesterly again.

After a run of half an hour, Charvey slowed as the train approached the little depot of Medgyesegyháza. For all practical purposes, the depot was Medgyesegyháza, with only a handful of dilapidated houses and sheds lining the roadway in front.

Charvey brought the train to a halt by a meandering creek's rickety bridge.

"We need water," he said, before Gideon could ask him why. "And I need a break and some food."

Gideon realized how hungry and exhausted he was. "Good idea," he said.

They walked along the trackbed, hearing the engine boiler wheezing softly. They climbed into László's private carriage.

Kinelly was dozing in an armchair. Eliska and In'Hout were sitting around a table sorting through a pile of papers, ID cards, permits, passports, and other documents.

"Where's Ian?" Gideon asked.

"Standing watch at the rear of the passenger car," Eliska said. She added, "I thought you'd stop eventually. I found the hampers of food Vilém had packed for the trip. Over there."

Gideon saw a plate heaped with spiced meatballs rolled in cabbage, and another of Bulgarian *revane* spongecake. He waited until Charvey and Brusilov filled plates, then started in himself.

"We have moved everything of value from the passenger compartments into this coach," Eliska said. "We found a strongbox of currency. A case of jewels. More ammunition."

Gideon looked around. He saw the material Eliska mentioned, next to trunks of clothing. Then his eye caught something that made him jump to his feet.

"Is that what I think it is?" he asked excitedly.

"If you mean a shortwave radio, yes," Eliska said. "That is how the priest informed us of your imprisonment in the small village."

Gideon turned to Brusilov. "I've got an idea how we can solve our problems at the border. Cutting red tape is exactly Philaix's cup of tea."

"Ah, I think I understand," Brusilov said.

Gideon picked up the radio and carried it outside. He extended a fourteen-foot telescopic aerial, adjusted the dial to a predetermined frequency, and cranked the handle. Once, a second time. Then a third and a fourth.

He glanced at his watch, keeping track of the time. If he had been in an urban area where German units roamed the streets tracking down illicit transmitters, he would have had to limit himself to a total transmission time of two and a half minutes. In this remote location, he thought he could permit himself more than that.

He cranked a fifth time. Then, to his jubilation, the set speaker crackled, "This is Base One, Phoenix. Over." The signal was faint, but just comprehensible.

Gideon spoke into the mouthpiece. "Phoenix to Base One. Urgent request for assistance. Over."

"Roger, Phoenix. Use Code B."

Gideon hesitated. There was a strong chance that the

Hungarian army would pick up the signal. But coding his message and decoding the replies would take too long. Gideon decided to communicate directly, in French. The Hungarians would have to translate the message, and that, he hoped, would give Phoenix time to get across the border.

"No code," Gideon said in French. Then he concisely summed up their location and situation.

The seconds swept by, Gideon impatiently checking his watch while he waited for a reply. Finally, the set speaker crackled again. Gideon moved his ear closer.

"Assume problem will be solved. Proceed to border." There was a pause, then a final, *"Bon chance."*

"Is that it?" Eliska asked. "How can he be so sure he can do something at four o'clock in the morning?"

"You don't know Philaix. A bloody genius," Kinelly said. For the terse Irishman, slow to praise anyone, the statement amounted to a ringing endorsement.

They headed back to the train, all feeling more optimistic than they had since they'd boarded the train at Debrecen.

As Gideon entered the salon of László's coach, Ian entered from the passenger coach and said, "I think you'd better come with me. I heard something."

"What is it?"

"Come."

Gideon followed, and Charvey came along behind him. When they reached the observation platform at the end of the last car, they could feel a slight vibration transmitting through the carriage trucks to their shoes. Charvey jumped down and put his ear near the rails. He could hear a definite humming noise.

He stood, urgency in his voice. "A train's coming behind us."

Gideon started. "Scheduled?"

"Not along this line," Charvey said grimly. Then without another word he turned and raced for the locomotive.

16

CHARVEY LEAPED INTO the locomotive and edged the tender under a barrel-staved tank. Gideon climbed up and carefully lowered the gooseneck pipe to the filler hole. Below, he could hear the scrape of coal as Brusilov began building up the fire.

He turned to look backward. To his dismay, he saw a single pinpoint of light moving toward him. "I can see the train," he shouted to Charvey.

"Let's get out of here," the Frenchman yelled back.

Gideon heard the couplers yank, and the train began to creak slowly forward. He jumped down out of the way. The gooseneck pipe of the water tank was ripped from the tender, then battered aside by the baggage car. Still pouring water, the spout scraped along the sides of the coaches. It was left behind, drowning the rails, while the train crossed over the rickety bridge and gradually built up speed.

Gideon came up to Charvey. "What do you think our chances are of outrunning whatever is behind us?"

"If they are in pursuit of us, they probably have a more powerful locomotive. Yet the poor condition of this branch line may work in our favor. It can barely support this relatively light engine and three cars at this speed. Greater weight would mean traveling more slowly. We should pick up some time."

"That would be nice," Gideon said, his voice weary. He looked out the window at the terrain, now a stretch of

149

dreary sandy hillocks interspersed with small stagnant pools. A flock of ungainly bustards flapped away, vanishing into the night. At the edge of the wetland, they passed through a stand of poplars and willows. Then the tracks began to rise.

Gideon turned his head to inspect the land behind them. The track was totally black.

"I can't see them," he said to Charvey. "We've pulled ahead."

"Good. That gives us time to try a last piece of deception. When we reach the next junction, I'll make a final attempt to put them off our trail."

That junction came ten kilometers down the line, crossing in the middle of nowhere. Charvey stopped the train after passing a switch marking an intersecting line. He swung out of the engine cab, and Gideon followed him to the tracks. They walked back to the switch they had just crossed over. Except for the hissing of the locomotive there wasn't a sound in the night stillness. The silence was comforting; for the moment, at least, they were alone.

Charvey moved the switch of the intersecting line. *"Regarde,"* he said, pointing to their line's mechanical signal. Each time he moved the intersecting train line's signal, the signal on their line moved oppositely. "For us to pass, the other signal must be red. That causes ours to be green. And tells anyone following us where we have gone."

"I think I see," Gideon said. "Now, we'll throw this one to green and they'll think we've taken it, since our line is red." Gideon paused for a moment, then asked, "But won't they be expecting us to switch the signals, especially since we have a lead on them?"

"Mais oui," Charvey answered, a mischievous grin appearing on his face. Then he reached out with both hands and in one powerful jerk snapped off the green wooden signal marker. "Come," he said to the now thoroughly confused Gideon. They both turned and ran ahead of the train to the red signal. Charvey snapped this off as well, then jammed the green wooden signal into the hole where the red had been.

"Got it," Gideon grinned.

"Good. Put the red signal back into the other slot. I'll get in the cab."

Moments later, Gideon hoisted himself aboard the locomotive. With a bellow of steam, the train moved on.

"The Hungarians are arrogant," Charvey said. "They'll believe we're fools. They'll see our clumsy signal switch and assume we have blundered."

Gideon laughed. "A double switch. Brilliant."

"I hope it is brilliant enough," Charvey replied.

The train picked up speed, taking them into a series of foothills rising from the plain. Siderodes flashing, wheel flanges screaming, the train spewed smoke and steam as it accelerated through a tiny junction, green signal eyes blurring past the windows. Gideon checked the name of the junction in a timetable and saw that they were less than an hour from the border.

The hills began to develop slopes and gullies, and the curves grew increasingly sharper. They were entering a spur of mountains. Charvey attacked the route with vigor, but, inexorably, the old locomotive started slowing as it struggled against the steepening grades.

Gideon decided to go back to the rear of the train. When he reached the salon, Kinelly and Ian were sitting at the table, carefully cleaning and checking the weapons. In'Hout, Eliska, and Brusilov paced like caged lions.

"This is the part I hate," Brusilov complained to Gideon. "Waiting, with nothing to do."

"I hope we've got nothing to do all the way across the border," Gideon said, starting back toward the passenger coach. Brusilov joined him.

They jumped the couplers and entered the coach. The bullet-shattered windows let in a moaning cold wind, and the only lights on were in the corridor. The place had an eerie feeling. A morgue, Gideon thought.

They quickly passed through to the observation deck at the rear.

"Not a good place to fire from," Gideon commented. "No cover at all."

"It doesn't matter," Brusilov said. "If a train of

soldiers gets close enough to shoot at us from the rear, we're in trouble, whether we have cover or not."

Gideon grimaced. He stood, ignoring the chill, watching the rails knife underneath as they sped through a series of compound curves.

Then he saw something, farther to the northwest, below the black corrugated ridges. He stared as it disappeared, his heart sinking. He had just nudged Brusilov when he saw it again. And now he was sure it was the beam of another train, maybe three kilometers behind them. And catching up fast. The trick hadn't worked.

Gideon said to Brusilov, "Go back and send Ian to tell Charvey the train's on our tail again." He paused, then added, "Not that he isn't doing all he can now."

Brusilov nodded, then went back into the coach.

Gideon continued to stare back. The first dim light of approaching dawn had turned the sky a dusky color. But the headlight behind still bored brightly into the night, growing in size at an alarming rate.

"They're going to catch us."

Gideon turned to see Eliska standing beside him. She looked pale and drawn.

"Probably," he said.

"What then?" she said, her voice betraying anxiety.

Gideon shrugged. "We fight them off the best we can. The way we always do."

"But if it's hopeless . . . If there are too many of them—"

"We'll have to head into those hills. Then try to make our way over the border."

A look of shock flashed across Eliska's face. "But what of the art? We've come so far. If there's the slightest chance . . ."

Gideon put his hands on her shoulders, realizing how much a part of Eliska's life was their precious cargo. "I think you know by now I'm not the kind of man who gives up easily. This mission was nearly impossible to begin with, and we've come damn close to pulling it off. But if we can't succeed, that's no reason to throw our lives away. There will be many other missions. This is going to be a very long war."

Eliska sighed, then closed her eyes for a moment. When she looked back at Gideon there were tears in her eyes. She said in a soft, sad voice, "It has already been a very long war."

Touched, Gideon kissed her on the forehead. Then suddenly came the unmistakable chatter of machine-gun fire. Gideon twisted the door open, pushed Eliska to the vestibule floor, then ducked in beside her. Looking back, he saw flashes from gun muzzles blinking against the brightening dawn. The pursuing train was bearing down on them.

When the train rounded a bend cut into the side of a narrow valley crag, bullets began raking its entire length. Keeping flat while he peered across the observation deck, Gideon saw the tracks behind them coiled in a horseshoe, which meant the two trains were running broadside with each other for a moment. The other train was being drawn by a 4-8-4 articulated-type "Express" locomotive, a Cadillac compared to their Model T Ford. The locomotive was propelling a flatcar ahead of it. On the flatcar was a squad of soldiers, blazing away across the canyon with old Great War tripod-mounted machine guns, strafing their train. Then another curve came along and the trains parted company.

Gideon took advantage of the lull in firing to grab Eliska's hand and help her to her feet. They dashed along the corridor, knowing their reprieve was only temporary. The track ahead, like that behind, was undoubtedly a series of switchbacks and hairpins which would constantly expose one or the other of their flanks to the swiveling machine guns. It was similar, Gideon thought sourly, to being the target of some man-of-war galleon making passes on the high seas. Sooner or later the rear of the train would be reduced to hash, or one of the coaches would disintegrate into smithereens. Or worse, the boiler plates would be punctured, and they'd be blown apart in a rupturing blast of scalding water and shrapnel.

And if the machine guns didn't get them, then the huge howitzer he'd spotted on the flatcar certainly would. It was an old field artillery piece, probably a French 75. Its awesome muzzle was trajectoried for ground level. Given a straight enough stretch to home in on the passenger coach, one shell would make mincemeat of them all. The Hungarians could damn well ram them with it, once their locomotive caught up. And at the rate it was going, it wouldn't take long.

The ledge at the front of the passenger coach reeled and yawed. Gideon poised as if bucking a storm-tossed ship deck, then leaped to the carriage, pivoting with one hand on the rung of its exit platform to lean back across and help Eliska. He clutched her around the waist, pulling her over and then inside the carriage. He ran with her along the sleeping-compartment corridor, furiously trying to figure a way out of the rapidly approaching disaster.

Urgency gripped him as the train curved once again into the open, this time on a steep incline which slowed the engine still more.

They raced into the salon, lead perforating the carriage's sides and riddling the interior all around them. Brusilov stood fearlessly at a window, firing his MP40 back at the flatcar in long, steady bursts.

"Ian's been hit," he shouted to Gideon. "Looks like just a crease across the scalp."

Gideon nodded grimly as he looked at the other men firing out the windows. They were obviously out of range with their weapons, laying out fire in a mad urge to fight back. The only effective fire would be from the observation deck. But with no cover on the deck, that was out of the question.

The observation deck . . . the passenger coach. That was it. The *coach*!

He started toward the rear of the carriage again, brushing past Eliska.

"Where are you going?" she cried.

"Stay here. And stay down," he called without stopping.

The low-throated hawking of the machine guns followed Gideon as he tore down the narrow corridor and out through the vestibule. Easing onto the narrow ledge outside the exit door, he looked down at the ties flashing by on the rails below. The two cars were grinding and

154

swaying erratically against each other, the coupling and air-brake hose wildly jerking back and forth.

He ran his tongue around his lips, aware of his parched throat. Then he lowered himself gingerly onto the carriage coupler, straddling it like a bronco, and began digging at the fastenings. The air-brake hose was first, a simple lever fitting. Except that there were two levers, one on each hose, requiring that they be squeezed tightly together like a nutcracker in order to break the connection. Gideon leaned over until his chin was resting on the passenger coach coupler, hands groping underneath. He pressed the levers together, his arms straining. At first he couldn't move them at all. Then slowly they inched closer together. With a violent hiss, the rubber hoses fell apart, trailing down and almost hitting the trackbed.

Gideon fought his way upright again, bullets ricocheting off the steel around him. The coupling was a pin-operated claw, stubbornly held in place by the inertia of the train. He wrestled feverishly at it, the pin resisting removal every inch of the way. He pulled with all his might, precariously maintaining his balance between the bucking train cars. Arms aching from the exertion, he felt the pin slowly begin to pull free. With a final jerk he yanked it up and out of the claw hinge, flinging it aside as he pivoted upward to clutch the rung for support.

A slug seared the shoulder of his coat, nicking his flesh, but he scarcely noticed it. He was focused now on the claw hinge, closed despite the pin's removal. "Open, damn you, open!" he raged at the coupling.

Impatient, half panicked, he kicked violently out at the coach. There was a scraping jolt, and the claw finally swung free. The old coach disengaged from the train and coasted to a halt on the upward grade. For a horrifying instant, he thought it might stay put. But then it slowly began rolling backward. It crawled at first, then gradually began picking up speed as it rumbled down the long curving section of track they'd just been climbing.

Gideon pulled himself onto the exit door deckplate, now out of the line of fire. He sat sucking in great lungfuls of air, watching the passenger coach careening out of control along the bend toward the flatcar. To his left rose the face of a massive ridge; to his right the tracks over-looked a jagged ravine. The coach teetered drunkenly, threatening to topple over before it reached the attacking train. And now the soldiers were aware of the hurtling menace. Sparks flew from the locomotive's driving wheels as brakes were hastily clamped on. The flatcar swayed violently as the train ground to a halt.

The passenger coach rocketed down relentlessly.

The soldiers were concentrating their machine guns on it, frantically trying to blow it off the tracks. The locomotive was reversing now. And the passenger coach plunged on.

Gideon held his breath.

The coach collided with the flatcar in a thunderous burst of wood and metal. It jerked sideways, the flatcar climbing over the coach's observation deck, both thrusting precariously out above the ravine as the soldiers were flung like rag dolls. There came a terrifying screech of wheels against the rails as the locomotive battled for its balance, but the hammering impact broke it loose as well.

Mashed together in corrugated wreckage, the coach, flatcar, and locomotive swayed for an instant on the ravine's brink. Then they began going over, flatcar first, then the coach and finally the great locomotive, smashing against boulders and brush, snapping towering fir trees. The cars bounced and rolled as they thundered down, cutting a ragged path like a giant wound. When they hit the rocky bottom, they exploded as one in a red ball of fire. Ammunition, especially the artillery shells, ignited with an ear-splitting roar that lit the predawn sky like a monstrous lightning bolt.

Up front, Charvey celebrated by tooting the whistle gleefully. Gideon slowly rose, grinning with relief. He gazed about, inhaling the sharp morning air. The awful beauty of the scene struck him. The hills outlined against the rosy sky, the evergreen-forested slopes and valleys, the graceful curve of the track behind him-and the luminescent wreck below, sending plumes of red and black upward from the canyon floor.

Charvey slowed the train to a stop. He came running back along the tracks, yelling, "Is everyone all right?"

"Yeah," Brusilov replied.

"*Mon Dieu*, that was a close one. The locomotive was on the verge of explosion. I don't think we can push her anymore."

"I hope we don't have to," Gideon said. "How far is the border?"

"Fifteen kilometers. Perhaps twenty. The grade is downhill, so it should be—"

He broke off abruptly. Gideon joined him in staring up at the sky, as a silver fighter plane screamed into view.

"God, no!" Charvey exclaimed.

Gideon stared. Then Ian was beside him with László's big field glasses to his eyes. He lowered them once, then put them back up as if to verify what his eyes had registered.

"What is it, Ian?" Gideon asked.

"A Messerschmitt. Luftwaffe markings."

"We had better get to cover, before we are strafed," Charvey said.

"No," Gideon said. "I don't think we're in that kind of danger."

"But why?"

"For one thing, the fighter would have made a pass by now if it were going to attack. We're right out in the open. I think the plane is up there to locate us, not shoot up the train."

"Why?" Ian asked. "The Hungarians were doing their best to blow us off the tracks."

"The Hungarians were primarily interested in stopping us. Revenge for our attack. The Germans want that art."

"What does that mean?" Charvey asked.

Gideon frowned. "I think it means we're going to meet a reception committee. Somewhere between here and the border."

17

An hour later, Gideon eased off the throttle bar and gradually applied the brake. The locomotive slowed to a stop on a small rise in the undulating plain that stretched to the outskirts of the border town of Szeged.

The azure sky was cloudless, and the rising sun, sitting like a white ball on the eastern horizon, bathed the switching yard a half kilometer ahead in soft morning light. It would have been a perfect scene, except for the five-car troop train, a German flag waving from the rear car, that blocked the single-track branch line. Flanking the train, on each side, was what looked to be at least a platoon of German SS troops.

Brusilov, who had been stoking the firebox, put down his shovel and wiped the perspiration from his face. Then he came up to Gideon and said, "You were right."

"Unfortunately, yes," Gideon said.

"What do we do now?"

"Nothing. We wait."

They didn't have to wait long. A German staff car drove through the line of troops toward them. The guidon of the III SS Division, the Death's Head badge of the Totenkopf SS, flew from the right front bumper. In place of the swastika that normally would be displayed on the left front bumper was a white flag.

Brusilov asked Gideon, "Do you think they're ready in the back?"

Gideon didn't respond for a moment, watching the staff

car move closer. Then he blew one long blast on the train's whistle.

The car came to a halt twenty yards from the train. "I think they came to talk," Gideon said. "But keep your hand near your weapon, just in case."

Brusilov nodded.

Gideon jumped from the cab, turned toward the car with arms raised to show he was unarmed, then waited.

A lean, broad-shouldered officer wearing the immaculate black dress uniform of an SS major stepped from the car. As he approached, Gideon inspected him carefully. He had a hard, handsome face with cold blue eyes that projected the authority of one long accustomed to immediate and unquestioned obedience.

The major came to a stop and stood in silence, surveying Gideon. When he spoke in German, his voice was cool and dispassionate. "I had hoped you would be an intelligent man. A man who recognizes that there is a time to talk as well as a time to fight."

"So talk," Gideon said brusquely.

The man's eyebrows rose. "Ah," he said, "a direct, blunt man. I should have expected as much from the leader of such a miraculously successful mission. I must congratulate you on your exploits, particularly the last one, your derailment of the Hungarian train. Very clever."

Gideon didn't respond.

The major flashed a cold smile, then continued, "Do not take your successes too much to heart, however. Your long journey is at an end. The track ahead, as you see, is blocked by our train. You are vastly outnumbered, should you foolishly choose to fight. And should you try to escape," he added, sweeping his hand across the flat, treeless expanse, "There is no cover. That is why I assume that, as a reasonable man, you will order your people to lay down their arms.

Gideon stared at him for a moment. Then he let a smile come to his face. "I request," Gideon said in a deliberately harsh, crude voice, "that you go fuck yourself."

Instant rage tightened the Nazi's face. "How dare you—"

Gideon interrupted him. "It's not us you're really after," he said, "it's that fortune in the train you've been sent to fetch. I can imagine your beloved Führer will be very pleased with you when he finds there's not a shred of canvas left that's big enough to wipe his ass with."

The SS major glared at Gideon. "What are you talking about?"

"Something that should have been obvious to an intelligent man like you," Gideon said sarcastically. "I've got that baggage car packed with explosives, all wired to go up at the first sign of an attack on the train."

"I see," the Nazi said, dispassion returning to his voice. "I must apologize for underestimating you. Of course, you realize that should those explosives be detonated, you and your men will perish."

"Better to go down fighting than let a Nazi pig like you get his filthy hands on us."

The color drained from the major's face. He was making an obvious effort to keep control. All traces of civility were gone from his voice when he asked, "What do you propose?"

"A deal. Our freedom for the contents of that baggage car."

"Of course," the major said. "I should have guessed. How do you propose this exchange be carried out?"

"I don't know yet," Gideon said. "I haven't had time to study the situation yet and figure out what kind of dirty tricks you're likely to pull. I'll need an hour to think about it."

"You will have an hour and no more," the major said. "And I insist that I be allowed to inspect the car to verify your claims."

"Forget it."

The major said, "Then there will be no deal." He turned and started to walk stiffly away.

Gideon let him get a few paces. Then he called out, "Okay. You can come inside."

The major beckoned toward the car. Two stormtroopers jumped out and trotted toward him, machine pistols in their hands.

"Wait a second," Gideon said, "I don't—"

"I am not going to be taken prisoner," the major said.

"Besides, I assume that you have taken a quick assault into your detonation plans. If there should be trouble, I'm aware that I would in all likelihood perish with you. And I can assure you I have no intention of doing that."

"All right," Gideon said. As he turned, he flashed a quick wink at Brusilov. Then he led the way toward the rear of the train.

The major started toward the front of the baggage car.

"Not that way," Gideon said. "All the way to the back."

They climbed up onto the observation deck of László's private coach. They went through the vestibule and started down the corridor. The major stopped after he glanced into the one lighted compartment.

Gideon took a step back to join him. The major was looking at two bodies lying on the floor. Both were dressed in black sweaters with the Phoenix emblem and black pants.

"You and your Hungarian buddies got two of my men," Gideon said harshly. "And you're damn sure not going to get any more. Just for those two I ought to—"

A high-pitched, short shriek came from the salon ahead.

"What's that?" the major asked.

"No! No! Not again," came the sound of a hysterical woman.

The major and his men pushed by Gideon and entered the salon.

Kinelly was standing menacingly over Eliska, his left hand raised, as if to strike her. She was huddled on the floor, weeping. Her blouse was torn in several places, exposing one breast. Her hair was wildly disheveled, there were scratches on her arms, and her right cheek bore the handprint from a blow.

When she saw the major, she cried, "Thank God." She scrambled toward him, half crawling. She threw her arms around his legs, saying, "Save me. I can't take any more."

The major's face registered shock. He swiveled his head toward Gideon. "I was prepared to respect you as a soldier. I now see proof that you're nothing but filthy animals."

Gideon looked at him with an arrogant smile. "She didn't mind fucking Count László. I can't see any reason why my men shouldn't have some fun."

The major's eyes narrowed. "There will be no deal unless this woman is allowed to accompany me."

Gideon pondered, then shrugged. "If you want her, we're through with her."

The major's lips tightened, but he held off a retort.

Gideon continued, "Now go inspect the baggage car. Remember, a flick of my man's wrist and it'll blow."

The major ordered one of the stormtroopers, "Go with him and see if it is as he says."

The major lifted Eliska to her feet. She clung to him, sobbing.

Gideon led the stormtrooper forward to the baggage car. When they returned, the soldier nodded to the major.

The Nazi officer said to Gideon, "You have precisely one hour."

"I'll pull the train forward then," Gideon said.

The major turned and started to help Eliska. She put her hand on his lapel and said, "Please. My coat. I'm so chilled."

"Of course," the major said. He motioned to a stormtrooper, who located Eliska's coat. It was draped around her shoulders, and they walked out of the car.

Kinelly came up to Gideon. "Bloody bastard fell for it."

"I was hoping he'd be one of the old-fashioned Prussian types. He had the proper sense of outrage."

"A monster with manners, eh?"

"Yeah," Gideon replied. Then he added, "Now we wait and see how successfully Charvey and In'Hout return from the dead."

In'Hout, dressed in drab peasant's clothing, pulled the horse cart to a stop. Across a wide field, he could see the smoke rising from the stack of the troop locomotive in the railroad yard.

"I thought we'd never get here," Charvey grumbled from the seat beside him.

162

"I couldn't go fast without attracting attention. Farmers move slowly."

"Well, we must act quickly. If we are late . . ."

"I know," In'Hout said grimly. He studied the terrain for a moment. "We could never make it across that field unobserved. I think we should continue on this road, then double back along the tracks from the south."

"That's where the yard workers are likely to be," Charvey said. "We should be able to surprise two of them and borrow their uniforms."

"Are you sure you can drive the locomotive of the troop train?"

Charvey looked offended. "But of course. I can drive anything. That is, if I'm not shot first trying to get into the cab."

In'Hout nodded, then snapped the reins to start the horse in motion.

Eliska's tension grew minute by minute as the clock moved slowly on. She paced back and forth in the salon of the staff car of the troop train, listening for the sound of the key in the lock that would indicate Major von Schiller's return.

That she had been locked in this room was not a good sign. Another bad sign was that forty-five minutes had passed since she'd left the train. Now she was afraid that von Schiller would not come to her at all before the hour deadline was reached. If he didn't come in five minutes, she had to try to break out.

Even if she did, she didn't know if she could fulfill her assignment—immobilizing the major. Her only weapon was the knife fastened to the inside of her coat sleeve. Without at least a pistol, she would be unable to storm the communications compartment of the car, where she assumed Major von Schiller was located. She had heard through the door the sounds of a telegraph clicking and the comings and goings of soldiers.

Eliska walked to the door, heard nothing, and sighed in exasperation. She ran Gideon's plan through her mind again. Charvey and In'Hout had slipped off the train a few kilometers back. Their job was to reach the cab of the troop train's locomotive and overcome the guards and crew. When Gideon moved his locomotive forward, Charvey was to move the troop train onto a siding, then disable the switch and the engine so that the troop train would be unable to pursue them the remaining four or five kilometers to the border.

Even if the train moved, of course, that left fifty armed soldiers flanking the track. Gideon hoped that if Eliska was able to take out the major, the lack of leadership would produce enough confusion for them to drive through the switching yard before the soldiers, with their crossfire, could react.

Gideon had admitted that the plan was a long shot. But it was their only hope, other than abandoning the train farther up the track. As long as the mission had any chance of success, however slight, Eliska could not have lived with that decision. She had volunteered for this part of the mission.

Her heart started beating faster as she heard steps in the corridor. She quickly sat in an armchair. A key turned in the lock and the door opened.

Eliska was disappointed to see that a young lieutenant was accompanying Major von Schiller. But she pulled herself together.

She rose and said to von Schiller, "Thank God you have not left me. I am so nervous after . . . after that nightmare. Horrible visions keep passing through my mind. I don't know if I can—"

Major von Schiller interrupted her with an expression of amused arrogance. "You can stop the histrionics now. I will not listen to more of this charade."

A jolt of fear went through Eliska. "Charade?" she asked in a hesitant tone. "I do not know . . ."

"The survivors of the attack on the Chapel of St. István reported a woman was a member of the raiding party. Their descriptions fit you perfectly. I doubt very much if you had been forced to wield a machine pistol with such deadly efficiency."

Eliska stared at him, unable for the moment to respond.

A thin smile appeared on the major's colorless lips.

"Good, no more words. You will listen. Whatever plan your leader has to get through our blockade will not work. Knowing the details, however, will save the lives of some of my men. Therefore, I request that you tell me the plans at once."

Eliska's eyes flashed defiance. "I will tell you nothing."

"Of course you will," the major said. "The only question is how unpleasant you would like to make the process."

Eliska glared at him. As she did so, her right hand moved up her sleeve to the handle of the knife, which was fastened so that the blade pointed up toward her shoulder. "So now you Germans torture women?"

"A female who kills forfeits the privileges of womanhood," von Schiller said. He ordered his aide, "Lieutenant Hoffman, seize her."

The SS officer moved forward, grabbing Eliska's shoulders. She suddenly bent her right arm. As the blade of her knife tore throught the sleeve at the elbow, she jabbed backward viciously.

The blade plunged deep under the rib cage of the lieutenant. He coughed once, staggered back a step, a look of almost comical surprise on his dying face. Then he fell to the floor, vomiting.

Major von Schiller leaped toward Eliska. She kicked out at him, her foot catching the inside of his thigh rather than the groin. The blow did cause him to stumble, giving her time to lunge for the door. She yanked the door open to find the gaping barrels of two machine pistols leveled at her.

From behind she heard von Schiller's angry command: "If that woman moves, cut her in half."

Two SS troopers blocked the dirt road, MP40s slung from their shoulder. Each had a pair of canvas MP40 ammo pouches attached to his black leather belt and stick grenades stuck into his belt and the top of each tall marching boot.

In'Hout halted the cart. As the soldiers approached, he quickly scanned the area. His eyes focused on two workmen with shovels digging by trackside about twenty yards away.

One of the soldiers barked to In'Hout in German. "This road is closed. Turn around."

In'Hout let a broad look of puzzlement come to his face, as if he didn't understand.

"Turn around," the soldier barked again.

In'Hout slowly turned and shot a look at Charvey, who shrugged his shoulders to indicate he, too, didn't understand.

The soldier grimaced in frustration. He turned and told his companion to grab the bridle of the horse to lead it around.

The moment the soldier turned his back, In'Hout leaped. The impact knocked the soldier to the ground, and before he could recover, In'Hout cut his throat.

The soldier standing in front of the wagon unslung his weapon. The muscular Charvey hurled a sack of grain at him. The sack hit the soldier in the chest, and he stumbled backward. Then In'Hout grabbed him from behind and slit his throat, too.

The two workman by the tracks had stopped to watch in stunned amazement. When they realized what was happening, they turned and started to run.

The two Phoenix team members were right after them. In'Hout, by far the fastest, caught up with the first workman in a few strides. He clubbed the man on the back of the head, then ran on. He tackled the second workman as he started to cross the tracks. They rolled in the cinders, wrestling desperately. Then Charvey arrived, waited his opportunity, and cracked the workman in the back of the head with a stone.

In'Hout got to his feet and stood by Charvey as they tried to catch their breath. Down the tracks a hundred yards was a switch, and beyond that the huge locomotive of the troop train on the main line. From where they were, In'Hout and Charvey could see two armed guards on either side of the locomotive.

In'Hout said to Charvey, "We'd better get into those soldiers' uniforms. It looks like we're going to need the firepower."

"And let us get moving," Charvey said. "The time, it is—"

Charvey suddenly pitched forward as the workman's shovel cracked into the back of his skull. In'Hout quickly spun and grabbed the shovel as the first workman, whom they'd assumed was down and out, aimed a blow at him. In'Hout pulled the workman toward him and punched him in the face. The workman fell, bleeding from the mouth.

In'Hout knelt by the unconscious Charvey. He slapped his face, saying, "Marcel. Marcel, wake up."

Charvey groaned but didn't open his eyes.

Then In'Hout heard the sound of a train whistle blasting in the distance. Once, twice, a third time.

In'Hout sighed in despair. That was Gideon's signal that the train was moving. He hadn't realized that the trip by horse cart had taken so long.

He turned his attention back to Charvey. There was no time left.

Gideon pulled the train to a halt ten yards from the rear car of the troop train. After the interminable hour of waiting, he was happy to be able to do something. The tension had drained his face of color when he turned to Brusilov and said grimly, "This is it."

Brusilov nodded.

Gideon moved to the left-hand door of the locomotive. He could see in front of him about twenty-five SS troops standing in one long single file facing the train, weapons in hand. Another group flanked the right side of the train.

Gideon was about to jump down from the cab. Then he saw the line of soldiers part and his heart sank. Eliska, hands tied behind her back, was being pushed along by an SS sergeant. Major von Schiller walked alongside.

Gideon exhaled sharply. Then he called out, "What is the meaning of this?"

Von Schiller smiled. "Your little deception has failed."

"Then I will blow up the baggage car," Gideon warned.

Von Schiller laughed. "Go right ahead and give the order. I have no more faith in your explosives than I had in the pathetic story of your spy."

Gideon stood in the doorway, his mind racing.

"Well?" von Schiller mocked. "Get on with it. Detonate the explosives."

Gideon glanced back at the baggage car. Ian and Kinelly stood in the entrance. Gideon grimaced, then looked silently back at the major.

"Just as I supposed," the major said. "Now I will tell you what you will do. You will throw down your weapons and step off the train into the open. Immediately."

Gideon stood unmoving. Then he heard a click behind him. Brusilov had disengaged the safety on his MP40.

Gideon turned to see a fierce glare in Brusilov's eyes. "I'm going to take some of those Nazi bastards with me," the Russian snarled.

"No," Gideon said. "We're doing as he says."

Brusilov's face registered shock, then anger. "I will not give in," he said. "Not for one second."

Gideon's voice was stern. "We'll throw down our weapons. That's a direct order, Avrahm."

Gideon watched the struggle reflected on Brusilov's face. In this desperate situation, nothing could command the Russian's obedience except the respect built up in the six months since Phoenix had been formed.

Never in thirty years of combat had the Russian surrendered to an enemy. He stood grim faced. Then the struggle was over. He walked to the door of the locomotive and tossed his weapon out onto the ground.

Gideon yelled back to Ian and Kinelly, who followed suit. They all climbed down from the train and stood together, ten yards from Major von Schiller.

Von Schiller said to Eliska, "Go. Join your friends."

She didn't move instantly. The sergeant prodded her in the back. She stumbled, then moved forward to Gideon's side.

Von Schiller inspected them, triumph on his face. Finally, he said, "Your miracles have been exhausted. Now you shall pay for your crimes against the Third Reich."

"The Geneva Convention states—" Gideon started.

"The Geneva Convention deals with soldiers in uniform, not spies and saboteurs," von Schiller said. "You are murderers. And you shall die now."

He motioned behind him. A squad of six soldiers moved up beside him, then knelt, putting the stocks of their MP40s against their shoulders.

Gideon saw Eliska trembling fiercely. He put his hand on her arm. "Steady," he said.

"It's been a bloody ball, mates," Kinelly muttered.

"Ready," Major von Schiller ordered.

Cartridges clicked into firing chambers.

A wave of despair flooded over Gideon. Then, summoning all his willpower, he steadied himself.

"Aim," came the command.

Gideon took a deep breath. Then, out of the corner of his eye, he caught the flash of the sun reflecting off a stick grenade flying through the air.

"Down!" he screamed, pulling Eliska with him as he dropped.

At that instant the firing squad unleashed a burst over their heads. A second later, the grenade detonated behind them, flinging bodies into the air. Then a .50 caliber machine gun opened up, raking the remaining line of SS troopers. They fell like toy soldiers under the withering impact of the steel-jacketed, heavy-caliber slugs. Gideon turned his head to see Major von Schiller, his black tunic drenched in blood, stagger a couple steps before pitching face down into the dirt.

Gideon sprang to his feet. Through the dust and smoke he caught a glimpse of Charvey swiveling the turrent-mounted machine gun as he continued to pour forth fire from the platform of the military vehicle parked behind the line of soldiers.

Gideon turned his attention to the other flank. He assumed that the MP40 chattering behind that line of soldiers was being wielded by In'Hout. Brusilov, faster than Gideon, had already leaped into the locomotive and was pouring out crossfire that was devastating the remaining Nazis.

Gideon gestured to Ian, then shouted, "Help Charvey get the locomotive. He's got to get the train out of the way so we can get the hell out of here."

Ian sprinted off, dodging and jumping over the corpses that littered the open ground. When he reached the military car, Charvey swung the machine gun around to rake the troop train. Three hundred rounds a minute slammed into the cars, shattering windows and stitching long ragged seams in the metal sides. From inside the sound of the horrible screams of the dying mixed with sporadic return rounds.

Ian tapped Charvey on the shoulder. The Frenchman looked at him, ripped off a final long burst, then picked up his MP40. "Let's go," he said to Ian.

They ran along the side of the train, weapons at the ready. A soldier appeared in the doorway of the command car, but Ian cut him down with a short blast.

As they approached the front of the train, Ian saw the gleam of a muzzle appear in the door of the locomotive. He dove under the train. Charvey followed, tumbling behind a huge metal wheel just as automatic-weapon fire clattered through the air.

Ian started to reach for a stick grenade he'd stuck in his belt. Charvey put his hand on his arm to stop him from pulling the string fuse.

"No," he said urgently. "We might cripple the train."

Ian crawled over to the right side of the train, debating. Then, to his glee, he saw In'Hout and Brusilov rushing toward the locomotive with weapons spitting fire. A return shot hit In'Hout in the shoulder, and he tumbled to the ground. Brusilov, ignoring the bullets, continued his mad rush. With a deafening bellow he plunged on, continuing to fire even after he leaped into the cab.

A moment later, there was silence. Ian looked out to see Brusilov waving them on. He nudged Charvey and then they were up and running.

When they reached the locomotive, they found the cab covered with blood and gore. Charvey pulled the body of a German soldier out by the legs, then climbed inside. Ignoring the body of the engineer, he checked the gauges.

"Ready to go," he announced. He told Ian, "You move forward and change that switch to the other track. When the train is past, change it back."

Ian ran off.

Back in his locomotive, Gideon was shoveling furiously, building up the fire to provide the speed they'd need to get across the border. Behind him, Eliska was cleaning the left side of Kinelly's face, which had caught some shrapnel from the blast of the grenade that had cut down the firing squad.

Gideon stopped shoveling when he heard the sound of a whistle. He dropped the shovel and moved to the front of the cab in time to see the troop train moving forward.

"Okay," Gideon said to himself. He released the brake of the locomotive. "Eliska," he yelled.

She anticipated him. "I'll shovel."

The train moved ahead with agonizing slowness. Gideon heard a shout. He turned to see Brusilov, who was carrying In'Hout in his arms as if he were a child. Gideon stopped the train momentarily to allow Brusilov to climb aboard, then started forward again.

Brusilov set In'Hout gently down and came up next to Gideon.

"How's Joel?" Gideon asked.

"Good enough," Brusilov replied. "But Charvey had better hurry."

Gideon caught the concern in his voice. "Why?"

"That Messerschmitt. It's coming back."

"Damn," Gideon spat. He turned his attention to the track ahead. The troop train was curving to the right, onto a northbound spur. Gideon halted his locomotive as he watched the cars one by one clear the switch.

Finally, the last car was on the siding. Ian pulled the lever and gave Gideon the thumbs-up sign. Gideon eased forward on the throttle, accelerating as Ian jumped on board.

Off to his right, Charvey had jumped out of the other locomotive and was sprinting toward them. When he'd gotten twenty yards away a blinding explosion rocked the engine, sending a huge plume of thick black smoke swirling into the blue morning sky.

Then, through the smoke of the blast, the Messerschmitt screamed into view on a terrifying strafing run. As the pilot hurtled toward them scarcely a hundred feet off the ground, he spotted Charvey, who had just gotten to his feet again. Twin machine guns opened up, churning the ground around the Frenchman.

"Run, Marcel!" shouted Brusilov.

Charvey raced toward them in a hail of fire.

As the rest of the team watched Charvey in anguished helplessness, Gideon jammed the throttle all the way forward. The engine shrieked in complaint, but the locomotive clanged ahead with enough increased speed that the machine-gun fire from the fighter raked the tender instead of the cab.

Hunks of coal and black dust flew everywhere. The plating of the boiler, no match for the heavier-caliber slugs of the plane's weapons, spouted water in a dozen places. With alarm, Gideon saw the steam-pressure gauge begin to drop.

Brusilov nudged him in time to see Ian helping Charvey climb into the cab.

Charvey took a moment to catch his breath, then moved forward to take over the controls.

"It's a miracle you made it through that fire," Gideon said.

Charvey grimaced. "It will be a miracle if this old beast carries us to the border. We've lost a lot of pressure. After another pass by that fighter . . ." He stopped, shaking his head.

Gideon looked out through the opening where the storm window had been. Ahead of them on the flat plain, they could see the barricades that marked the border a couple kilometers ahead. Three or four minutes and they'd be across.

Gideon glanced off to the southeast. The Messerschmitt, a silvery dot in the blue sky, was completing a circle that would catapult it into another deadly dive. Gideon was about to turn away when he saw a cluster of other dots moving toward the Messerschmitt.

Gideon pointed with a finger and said to Brusilov, "More trouble. He's got help."

"I do not think so."

"What do you mean?"

"Those planes are approaching from south of the border. There are no German aircraft stationed in Yugoslavia. Those must be Yugoslav fighters."

"You're right," Gideon said enthusiastically.

The Messerschmitt, however, had started its run. It was boring in on them, screaming out of the sky. Gideon's whole body was tense as he saw the four Yugoslav fighters racing in at an angle, trying to cut the Messerschmitt off.

No way, Gideon thought, there's not enough time. The noise of the Messerschmitt could now be heard clearly over the chugging steam engine, as its machine guns started to spit fire.

Then the leading Yugoslav fighter sent a hail of bullets streaming in front of the Messerschmitt's nose. The German machine guns abruptly stopped. The Nazi pilot must have jerked his head to his left, in spite of the fact that his plane was racing along perilously close to the ground.

The German plane dropped. It cleared the locomotive with less than fifty feet to spare. Gideon swiveled in time to see the plane slam nose first into the ground.

Gideon watched a ball of smoke and flame erupt like a volcano. He was so transfixed he didn't notice the locomotive slowing.

They'd crossed the border.

"Philaix, he must have some powerful connections in Yugoslavia," Charvey remarked.

Gideon, seeing the triumphant smiles blooming on the faces of his comrades, grinned broadly in return. "We made it," he said.

Here's the first chapter from SHADOWS OF DEATH, the third action-packed book in the RESISTANCE series —about the Phoenix team's newest mission. . . .

RESISTANCE 3: SHADOWS OF DEATH

1

THE FRESH WIND raised a chop on the water, flicking a fine spray over the Havre trawler as it tacked to port against the heading seas. Although the date was July 10, the water of the English Channel was ice-cold. Despite a thick woolen sweater, skullcap, and pea coat, Scott Gideon was thoroughly chilled. He sat on the deck with his back against the gunwale next to a stacked net of knotted manila hemp that helped cut the wind a bit. He tried to force his mind off the long, unpleasant crossing and onto the mission ahead.

Deep in thought, he didn't notice Charvey standing in front of him until the Frenchman said, "Gideon. Do you hear?"

Gideon stood. For a moment his ears caught only the slap of the waves against the bow. Then the low hum registered, and he tensed.

When he looked around, he saw the others were alert. Eliska and In'Hout stood near the bow, scanning the seas. Brusilov crouched amidships, his hand resting on the wooden fish barrel that contained the Sten submachine guns. Only the helmsman, an old French fisherman, sat as calmly as before on a thwart across the stern, his gnarled hand resting on the tiller as he studied the nuances of the wind.

That wind was nearly twenty knots now, and played such tricks with the sound that Gideon couldn't tell from what direction the hum was coming.

Then Charvey pointed toward the leaden sky. "Planes," he said. "Coming from France."

The droning was louder now, and Gideon realized Charvey was right. Unseen above the thick cloud cover was obviously a sizable formation of aircraft.

Gideon was relieved. "We can't see them, but they can't see us, either. I was afraid the sound was a German E-boat."

"Out here?" Charvey asked.

Gideon grimaced. "They've got a range of seven hundred miles and a top speed of nearly forty knots an hour. Even if we heard the boat, we might not see anything except the bubbly trail behind a torpedo before it blows us to smithereens."

"Les Boches!" Charvey spat contemptuously. "So arrogant. Their propagandists, they call them the gods of war. I cannot wait to reach land. Then the blood of many gods will be on my hands."

Gideon looked for a moment at the squat, dark, muscular Frenchman. During the previous Phoenix commando missions in Poland and Hungary, Charvey's dry wit had done much to relieve the tension of operating in enemy territory. But since the fall of France three weeks before, the former Parisian trade unionist had become grim and bitter.

Charvey continued to stare upward for a few moments. Then he exhaled and said to Gideon, "The Brits. They are in for it, eh?"

"The last intelligence reports I read showed that the Germans have seventeen hundred bombers and eight hundred fighters in northern France. The British have about five hundred fighters to try to shoot them down."

"Mon Dieu!" Charvey exclaimed. "What chance do they have?"

Gideon shrugged. "They've got a tough go of it," he said. "But no chance at all if our mission fails." He paused for a second, then added, "Talk to our chauffeur, will you? I'd like to know when he thinks we'll reach Cherbourg."

Gideon watched Charvey move toward the stern. Then he sat back down on the deck, his mind on the last briefing by H. Auguste Philaix, the wealthy Belgian industrialist who had both founded and bankrolled the elite Phoenix commando team. The base for their first missions had been Philaix's palatial estate in Belgium. But since the Nazi *Blitzkrieg* against the West, begun two months before on May 10, 1940, Philaix had set up headquarters in an English country estate, Bladesover Manor, in Oxfordshire, forty miles from London. A week before, in the library of the imposing gray stone house, Philaix had told Gideon—leader of Phoenix—about Sir Arnold Burrington and the "black box."

"Sir Arnold," Philaix had explained, "is one of Britain's most distinguished physicists. He was one of the key members of a top-secret scientific team working on a more effective form of radar. Are you familiar with radar?"

Gideon had nodded. "Sure. Pulses of electromagnetic waves broadcast by a directional antenna. Any object the waves reflect from, like an airplane, is picked up by a receiver."

"Just so. With the threat of war, it became obvious that a better transmitter was needed, one that could broadcast shorter wavelengths for more accuracy and use more power to increase range. Very recently, Sir Arnold's group came up with a major breakthrough—a device called the cavity magnetron, or, more colorfully, the 'black box.' This machine not only provides more accuracy and range, it also allows the construction of radar sets small enough to be mounted inside aircraft and surface naval vessels. The advantage that provides to an outnumbered air force and a fleet riddled by U-boats I do not have to describe."

Gideon had replied, "But if the British have this magnetron already, what's our job?"

An even grimmer expression came onto the face of the dour Belgian. "In early May, Sir Arnold and three colleagues came to Belgium with blueprints of the magnetron. They and my people discussed manufacturing these black boxes at my electronics complex in South Africa, far from the war zone. Sir Arnold left for home by train a day before the German attack. Unlike myself, however, he suffered complications. His trip ended in Paris."

Gideon's eyebrows raised. "You mean the Germans have him?"

"I do not know. All I have is a short communication and a Paris address. You and your team will go to Paris, destroy the blueprints, and bring home Sir Arnold and his colleagues."

"What if they're in German hands?"

"You extricate them," Philaix ordered. "If they have been sent on to Germany, you follow them. The fate of the British nation may well hang in the balance."

The next seven days had consisted of round-the-clock briefings and preparations. It had been a relief to finally drive away from Bladesover Manor.

In fact, the trip had started more like a summer excursion than a dangerous mission. After leaving the train at Plymouth, the Phoenix team had traveled by touring car on a narrow, winding Cornwall road lined by tall hedgerows that hid the digging-in, camouflaging, and other preparations for the invasion the British feared could come at any time. In early evening, they'd reached Fowey, a tiny fishing village clinging to the steep shore of the harbor. In the pale, clear light, the slender deepwater anchorage filled with ketches, old yawls, trawlers and sloops seemed as timeless and peaceful as a postcard.

Gideon's feeling of serenity had continued even after they loaded their weapons and other gear on the French fishing boat and left the mooring. As the trawler's old two-cycle gas engine sputtered and coughed, propelling the boat through the harbor, Gideon had looked back to see the stunning panorama of the village and the surrounding hills illuminated in the burning red light of sunset. The scene took him back to the many nights of his boyhood in Oswego, New York, sitting after supper on the porch of his large Victorian home, watching the sun sink slowly and lazily into the blue waters of Lake Ontario.

Then the sky, like the coals of a fire, had faded from red to gray. The trawler passed through the mouth of the harbor, a slash in the high coastal cliffs. As Gideon and the rest of the team had rushed to hoist the two lug sails and the jib, the clouds had thickened. The wind picked up and the horizon seemed to creep closer. The wooden boat became a tiny speck in a vast, cold, alien universe.

The English Channel was in fact alien territory. Across the narrow body of water that the British were calling "the largest anti-tank ditch in the world" were poised 136 German divisions. The Channel was a no-man's-land, a sea and air battleground as deadly as the ground between the trenches in World War I.

Gideon needed to get across the Channel before dawn. The odds against five people filtering through the entire German occupation force were high enough without being trapped out in the open in daylight like ducks on a pond.

Gideon glanced at his watch. A little after two in the morning. His muscles were stiff from the cold and the tension. He got to his feet to check on his men.

Or, rather, he reminded himself as he moved around stumpy wooden barrels of herring to make his way to the bow, his men and the woman.

Eliska Dobrensky was sitting on top of the gunwale, holding onto a halyard as the bow rose and fell. Her delicate features, framed by the dark scarf she wore, made her look as exquisitely beautiful as the aristocratic young ladies portrayed on miniatures in the National Gallery of Art.

"Hear anything?" Gideon asked.

"I hear many things," she replied. "The wind is howling so, there are many strange sounds."

"You're right," Gideon said. He was aware now that the swells pushed by the wind had become wilder, and above him the sails flapped and snapped as the helmsman struggled to adjust to the gusts.

Eliska spoke again. "In Czechoslovakia we have no experience with the sea. Yet I find that it—"

The shrill whine of a klaxon cut through the night like a knife. A cold chill ran through Gideon. The siren sounded again, a longer blast.

Gideon swiveled his head back toward Eliska. "German torpedo boat," he said. "Close by. You ready?"

She grabbed a satchel at her feet, tightened her life jacket, then nodded.

Gideon pushed her over the side of the boat. He turned around just as the spotlight came on. The beam was blinding, and Gideon couldn't see a thing. He hoped to hell In'Hout, Charvey, and Brusilov were at their assigned stations, looking as much like French fishermen as possible.

Gideon, despite the gale, could now hear the increasing roar of the torpedo boat's twenty-cylinder V-form Daimler-Benz diesel. Over the sound of the engine came the voice of an officer using a bullhorn. "Lower your sails. Lower your sails."

Another shock went through Gideon. The announcement was made in English. His hope of a cursory inspection was shattered. The crew of the German boat was suspicious and ready for a thorough search.

Gideon could hear the French helmsman unleashing a string of curses. Then the same announcement was made in slow, poor French. The searchlight swung away, illuminating the choppy water off the bow. After taking a moment to let his eyes adjust, Gideon started to furl the jib.

The fisherman swung the trawler abeam to face upwind, spilling air from the sails so they could be lowered more easily. Over his shoulder, Gideon could see Charvey, In'Hout, and Brusilov working on the lugs. He furled the jib, folded it, then leaned against the gunwale with the sail in his lap.

The throbbing of the diesel engine muted, and the torpedo boat came up alongside, drenching the trawler with icy spray. Gideon cursed, wiped his face, then looked over to inspect the boat in the reflected glare of the spotlight.

The E-boat looked as big as a destroyer next to the trawler. Four times as long as the thirty-foot fishing vessel, with a draw of less than five feet, it loomed over the wooden boat, the wheelhouse like a perch ten feet above the Havre trawler's gunwales.

This class of boat, Gideon had been told, carried a crew of twenty-one men. He could see gunners stationed at the 20mm Spandau machine guns mounted on the bow and stern. Four sailors armed with MP40 machine pistols were fore of the wheelhouse, another four aft. Gideon could make out at least five heads in the wheelhouse— probably the captain, first officer, boatswain, navigator, and helmsman. Below, he was sure, were the men who loaded the torpedos that were fired from the 21-inch tubes pointing forward from high on each side of the bow. Also below were the mechanics.

Gideon was staring at the bow when the torpedo boat bumped the trawler. Four armed sailors jumped down to the fishing boat's deck, followed by an officer holding a Luger.

As the officer came into the beam of the spotlight, Gideon could see on his hat and right breast the eagle and swastika badge of the Deutschen Kriegsmarine, the German navy. The officer moved with the typical rigid, arrogant, swaggering walk of a fanatical Nazi.

The officer waved to his men. One started toward the bow, poking at piled fishing nets and canvas with the barrel of his weapon. He came up to Gideon, surveyed him for a moment, then with a swift move tore the jib sail out of his hands.

Gideon's hands were empty. He fought a smirk, trying to keep his face a mask of servile sullenness.

Another sailor came up to Brusilov, who was sitting with his hand on the top of the sail box. The sailor motioned for Brusilov to move his hand. The huge Russian just stared at him dumbly. The sailor slammed the butt of his weapon on Brusilov's hand.

Brusilov jumped up, howling in pain. Gideon sensed trouble, but the Russian just glared, holding his hand as the sailor opened the lid of the sail box. The officer came up beside him, inspecting the inside with the flashlight.

Charvey came up beside the officer. "Please, *mon capitaine*," Charvey said. "We are but poor fisherman. We mean no harm."

The officer whirled to face him. "Where are the weapons?" he demanded harshly.

A look of amazement came to Charvey's face. "Weapons? We have no weapons."

"I will blow this boat out of the water unless you tell me."

"Search," Charvey said. "We have nothing to hide."

The officer studied him for a moment. Then he asked, "Where are you from?"

"Île de Bréhat."

"Out this far?"

Charvey shrugged. "Since the war, food is so scarce. We must follow the big schools, to feed our people. The herring, they run far."

The officer walked over to a wooden barrel and pried off the lid. He stared down at the herring packed into the briny water. He reached his hand in, felt around, removed his hand, and started to turn back to Charvey.

Gideon breathed a quiet sigh of relief. Then the officer whirled and kicked over the barrel. Fish and water spilled out all over the deck. The officer shone his light down. The beam reflected off the long, lumpy wrappings of the Stens and grenades.

"Saboteurs," the officer said with triumph in his voice. "You shall all die for this."

Gideon took a step forward. But the barrel of a weapon jammed into his stomach stopped him.

The weight of her satchel pulled Eliska underwater after she tumbled backward off the boat. Then the life jacket yanked upward. The trawler had moved slightly to port, and she rose underneath it, cracking the back of her head on the keel. Everything was dark for a moment, though she thought her eyes were open. She bobbed above the surface, tried to breathe, but the salt water filled her nose and mouth and stung her eyes. Dizziness flooded over her.

When the dizziness subsided, she scanned the seas. She was ten yards from the fishing boat spotlighted in the vast dark Channel. She was exhausted, but fear motivated her and she started to swim.

In the choppy water, she seemed to make no progress, the waves pushing her back as far as each stroke took her forward. When she paused for a rest, she saw the torpedo boat coming up next to the trawler. A new urgency came over her and she started swimming again with arms and legs that throbbed painfully.

To her relief, the boats started drifting toward her. With hard work, she ducked under the shadow of the fishing boat seconds before a flashlight beam swept the open water from which she'd come.

She rested a moment, trying to remember what Gideon had told her. The intense cold was starting to numb her mind as well as her body. It came to her slowly, as if she were drugged. "Move around the bow," Gideon had said. "Don't try to swim under the torpedo boat. There are three propeller shafts that would cut you to ribbons."

She took a last deep breath, then pushed off from the trawler. She made her way around its bow, then smacked into the torpedo boat at the waterline. Her satchel hit the metal, producing a ringing sound that to her was as loud as a church bell. She held her breath, waiting to be discovered.

But all she heard was snatches of shouting from the boat. She knew time was getting short, so she pushed off again and finally made her way around the bow of the torpedo boat to the starboard side, the side away from the trawler.

With fingers she could barely feel, she pulled the first of the magnetic mines from the satchel. As quietly as she could, she affixed it just below the waterline near the bow. By feel, she turned the fuse the distance she'd practiced hundreds of times. Then she moved amidships and placed a second mine as high as she could beneath the torpedo tube.

Then she dropped the satchel, kicked off from the boat, and began to swim. The first fuse was set for three minutes, so she had to hurry. But her arms were like lead. The bow of the trawler seemed miles away.

The German officer reared back and struck Charvey across the face with his Luger. The Frenchman staggered back, spitting blood.

"Who are you?" the officer roared. "What are you doing?"

Charvey didn't respond.

The officer struck him again. He fell to his knees.

The officer turned to his men. "We will take one on

183

board for questioning." He looked around, then pointed to the slender Joel In'Hout, "That one. We will shoot the others and sink the boat."

"But there may be more weapons," one of the men said.

"We do not have time," the officer said curtly. "We must resume our patrol, or else—"

At that instant, the first mine exploded with a muffled boom. The torpedo boat lurched violently, slamming broadside into the fishing boat.

The officer tumbled backward, hit the port gunwale, and fell into the water. The jib boom swung around, cracking the skull of the sailor near Gideon. As the sailor dropped unconscious, Gideon dove for his weapon. In one smooth, swift motion, Gideon pulled it to firing position and triggered a burst toward the bow Spandau gunner. A crimson line was stitched across the gunner's chest as he staggered two steps and tumbled over the rail.

Gideon swept his fire toward the four men fore of the wheelhouse. He was joined by Brusilov, who'd smashed the skull of a sailor against the mast and swept up the weapon that now bucked and kicked in his massive hands, pouring a drenching hail of fire at the wheelhouse. Glass shattered and bodies flew as agonized screams filled the air.

Marcel Charvey grabbed at the weapon of the sailor closest to the stern. The Nazi hung on, and they grappled as the fishing boat dipped deep into a swell. The German kicked out, then pulled hard as Charvey lost his balance. The sailor wrenched the weapon free, but the rising motion of the trawler tossed him over the gunwale into the sea.

Charvey looked around for another weapon. Then he lunged for cover as the rear Spandau gunner opened up, raking the stern of the trawler. The French fisherman screamed as steel-jacketed slugs tore through him. He jerked like a puppet on a string, then fell into a pool of his own blood as Charvey watched helplessly.

The 20mm machine gun continued to pour out a torrent of heavy-caliber fire that ripped to splinters the tiller and the thwart on which the helmsman had been sitting.

Then the gunner swiveled his weapon to saturate the midships area of the fishing boat.

The torpedo boat was now listing to starboard, and Gideon and Brusilov huddled out of the firing line on the starboard side of the trawler. They watched helplessly as the machine-gun fire tore apart the lug rigging and cut down the masts.

"We've got to get that guy," Gideon shouted. "That other mine will go off any second. If the torpedoes inside detonate, we'll be goners, just like the E-boat."

"I'll climb on board the German ship," Brusilov said, "then see if I can make my way back."

"I've got a better idea," In'Hout said. The Dutchman had crawled up to Gideon's side. "Give me some covering fire."

"Wait a—"

In'Hout moved out low and hard toward the stern. Bullets churned up the deck around him before he dove behind the fish barrel the German officer had kicked over. The Spandau gunner directed fire at the barrel, which started to disintegrate as In'Hout stretched out a hand and pulled in one of the waterproof bundles lying amid the herring. Slivers of wood tore into his skin as he fumbled at the rope. Finally, the rubber fell open, revealing six hand grenades. In'Hout pulled the ring to fuse one, then stood. Ignoring the intense fire, he took careful aim and threw the grenade. Bullets continued to gnaw around him as he dropped back to the deck.

The grenade detonated with a loud boom, hurling the gunner into the Channel. Then there was an eerie silence.

The silence didn't last long. Gideon yelled to Charvey, "Get that motor started and get us out of here." He turned to Brusilov and started to say, "Let's push off the—"

"Help!" came the cry.

"Eliska!" Gideon shouted. He rushed over to help her into the fishing boat.

Charvey dashed to the stern and punched at the starter of the balky engine, once, twice, then a third time. On the fourth try, the engine sputtered, then stopped.

"*Merde!*" Charvey swore. He punched the button again and held it down.

The engine kicked to life. Charvey reached back for the tiller, then realized it was gone.

"Hurry," Gideon shouted.

Charvey engaged the gears. The wind and waves were pushing the trawler into the listing torpedo boat. The wooden vessel banged against the steel hull repeatedly. Charvey put the throttle on full. For an instant the rich fuel-and-oil mixture almost choked off the motor. Then the fishing boat lunged free and plunged erratically into the dark night.

Charvey watched the torpedo boat fade from view. Then, a split second before the roar hit his ears, he saw the Nazi craft disintegrate in a blinding orange-white ball of flame.

Charvey hit the deck as shards of metal flew overhead. A shock wave lifted the fishing boat like a toy, and the boat flew through the air, slamming into the water with shuddering force.

It was a few moments before the members of the team pulled themselves together and got to their feet. The shivering, soaking wet Eliska clung to Gideon as she stared back into the blackness where the E-boat had been. "I did not think we would escape," she said.

Gideon didn't reply right away. Finally he said, "We're not out of the woods yet. Look around."

Eliska became conscious of angry gusts of wind that were cutting the tops off the wave crests, flattening them. The boat was bucking like a bronco, buffeted by the seas.

"A squall," Gideon said. "And we're without a helmsman. Not to mention a tiller."

JOIN THE <u>RESISTANCE</u> READER'S PANEL

If you're a reader of <u>RESISTANCE</u>, New American Library wants to bring you more of the type of books you enjoy. For this reason we're asking you to join the <u>RESISTANCE</u> Reader's Panel, so we can learn more about your reading tastes.

Please fill out and mail this questionnaire today. Your comments are appreciated.

1. The title of the last paperback book I bought was:
   TITLE: _____ PUBLISHER: _____

2. How many paperback books have you bought for yourself in the last six months?
   ☐ 1 to 3   ☐ 4 to 6   ☐ 7 to 9   ☐ 10 to 20   ☐ 21 or more

3. What other paperback fiction have you read in the past six months?
   Please list titles: _____
   _____
   _____
   _____

4. My favorite is (one of the above or other): _____

5. My favorite author is: _____

6. I watch television, on average (check one):
   ☐ Over 4 hours a day ☐ 2 to 4 hours a day ☐ 0 to 2 hours a day
   I usually watch television (check one or more):
   ☐ 8 a.m. to 5 p.m.   ☐ 5 p.m. to 11 p.m.   ☐ 11 p.m. to 2 a.m.

7. I read the following numbers of different magazines regularly (check one):
   ☐ More than 6   ☐ 3 to 6 magazines   ☐ 0 to 2 magazines
   My favorite magazines are: _____
   _____

For our records, we need this information from all our Reader's Panel Members.

NAME: _____

ADDRESS: _____

CITY: _____ STATE: _____ ZIP CODE: _____

8. (Check one) ☐ Male   ☐ Female

9. Age (check one): ☐ 17 and under   ☐ 18 to 34   ☐ 35 to 49
   ☐ 50 to 64   ☐ 65 and over

10. Education (check one):
    ☐ Now in high school   ☐ Graduated high school
    ☐ Now in college   ☐ Completed some college
    ☐ Graduated college

11. What is your occupation? (check one):
    ☐ Employed full-time   ☐ Employed part-time   ☐ Not employed
    Give your full job title: _____

Thank you. Please mail this today to:

RESISTANCE, New American Library
1633 Broadway, New York, New York 10019

More SIGNET Adventure Stories